CYANIDE CONSTELLATIONS:

AND OTHER STORIES

Copyright © 2025 Sara Tantlinger

A note about reprints can be found on page 181.

Edited by Rob Carroll
Book Design and Layout by Rob Carroll
Cover Art by Devin Forst
Cover Design by Rob Carroll

Library of Congress Control Number: 2025946800

ISBN 978-1-958598-81-8 (paperback)
ISBN 978-1-958598-12-2 (eBook)

darkmatter-ink.com

CYANIDE CONSTELLATIONS:

AND OTHER STORIES

SARA TANTLINGER

CONTENTS

THE VIRIDESCENT DARK

Ana had no rational reason to feel uncomfortable. Yet, unease filled her chest as if a boulder had replaced her heart. The weight of anxiety might've made sense if the den had windows. At least then, she could tell herself the feeling stemmed from the paranoia of someone peeking through open blinds.

Maybe that's the problem, she thought. No windows. Her and her husband had turned the den into a library they both loved, but after a night of its absence, natural light would be a welcome visitor in the morning hours. Blake even built the wooden shelves himself, and together they'd spent countless hours arranging too many books in alphabetical order. The den was their curated place of idyllic happiness. Seclusion, books, and each other.

Still, Ana felt watched. Something lurked on the other side of the wall. Beyond the paneling waited a lively forest, full of summer wildlife and tangled fauna. The trees kept the small house hidden from the nearest road. A passerby would have to be pretty brave to take the turn off the main road and travel up their uneven driveway.

A gut feeling or intuition, some primal part of her brain recited a warning: *Do not go out there.*

She glanced at the clock on the wall, surprised it was almost midnight. Blake had already gone to bed. Their gray, short-haired cat, Walt Whisker, had followed him as usual, and Ana wished she had, too. She could go wake her husband, or crawl under the covers, but instead she picked up her phone. Nothing like an aimless social media scroll for distraction.

Missed calls and texts filled her lock screen. Her hand froze in the air as her heart sped up into a pounding rhythm. That many missed messages usually meant someone she loved was dead. She'd left the phone on silent for the past few hours while reading, and it seemed like everyone she'd ever met had left a message.

"What the hell?"

The anxiety boulder in her chest shook. Fractured. Threatened to explode and send shards of rock to pierce her skeleton. With trembling fingers, she unlocked the phone but couldn't bring herself to click on the voicemails or texts. Some thoughtless part of her gave into habit, opened up Instagram without really thinking. There was no reason why she should ignore the messages and open a stupid app instead, but she did. The action lacked explanation, just as she couldn't explain why she both needed and did not need to go outside. To see what lingered on the other side of the wall.

The same post displayed on her screen. Over and over. Photos and reels of a silver-green orb filled her feed. Similar pictures from different angles, with varying levels of clarity. A blurry haze, tinted emerald, framed the bright orb. As Ana scrolled through the posts from a range of timestamps, realization pierced her like fangs sinking into her brain.

A familiar orb with craters, hovering in the darkness. What had happened to the moon to make it look so sick?

Within a few short hours, the green had expanded. A post from 9:00 p.m. showed visible specks of green polka-dotting the moon. The most recent post, from a few minutes ago, presented the moon with nearly half its surface covered, like moss or a strange forest. The hellish haze glowed stronger, beaming an emerald aura down to Earth. Ana zoomed in, spotted other hidden colors. Streaks of red and brown and black.

A numb panic took hold; the whole affair was too unbelievable for her mind to process. Captions and comments repeated similar sentiments of disbelief. People said goodbye to one another. They confessed secrets and sins. Shared dreams and wishes never to come true.

The rest were theories of what caused the moon to turn viridescent.

"What does it matter?" Ana whispered to the room. No explanation would stop whatever had come to plague the moon.

Despite her numbness, she almost laughed. The whole situation bordered on absurdity. Of course she'd learn about some freakish event through social media. It was more than an abnormality, though.

She'd read the article weeks ago and moved on, like everyone else. A scientist had gained brief internet fame for an eloquent piece stating a change to the moon would soon arrive. *The beginning of the end*, he had called it.

The end of the world. *Impossible.*

A kind of delirium consumed Ana. She set her phone down next to the book she'd abandoned and walked toward the porch door. So many hours had been spent out there, sitting with Blake in the evenings. She'd read him a passage in a book she liked, and he'd recite a poem from memory for her. His warm voice would fill the night as she gazed at the stars. They both worked hard to earn the beauty of those moments. How could it all disappear?

Fingers moved the lock to the left, unlatching the porch door. She moved robotically, muscle memory guiding her out onto the concrete. Her tomato plants and potted flowers glowed beneath the sickly haze, as if radiation lit the night. That's not what this was, though. Whatever the moon emitted, it was something new.

Strange dust clung to the porch furniture, lustrous against the off-white cushions. She stepped closer, an ache budding in her to reach out and touch the powder.

"Ana?" Blake's voice. The gentle sound of it nearly brought her to tears.

She stood still, halfway between the door and the sooty chair. "Stay inside."

"You should take your own advice."

"I think it's too late," she said, her eyes meeting his gaze once before she realized the dust had already fallen on her bare arms. It satisfied the curious ache, and she moved away from the small pile of green pollen collecting on the cushions. Her right pointer finger dabbed at the substance on her left arm, and she swabbed it around her skin like testing a swatch of eyeshadow.

"Stop," Blake said and took a step forward, but he lingered in the doorway, not venturing outside. "Ana, don't."

The fear in his tone, his concern… It broke her heart. She loved him more than anything in this life, but how could love save them?

"Please come back inside."

She drifted toward him and moved willingly when he put a gentle arm around her waist, guiding her toward the kitchen after he shut and locked the porch door. He was careful, she noticed, not to touch her skin, and had used the sleeve of his overshirt when he guided her away from the door.

Blake unbuttoned the overshirt and threw it in the trash. "We don't know what that stuff is."

She nodded and moved to wash off the dust from her arms and hands. Despite her scrubbing, a faint stain remained.

"Here." Blake had disappeared and returned with a new shirt and pants for her. She accepted the clothes, changed, threw the supposedly contaminated ones in the trash like he had done. Every movement felt like going through the motions. Ana had always prided herself on being in touch with her emotions, and with being able to honestly communicate with her husband. Now, she wasn't sure how she felt at all. Curious. Maybe sad. Maybe so hopeless she'd gone numb.

"Look at the windows." Blake's voice had gone even quieter.

Fear. She recognized that emotion clearly as she took in the mossy smears on the window. Green covered the glass. Where a speck started, it then stretched with wriggling tendrils, and quickly took over the surfaces around it. Like something sentient.

Ana looked away and focused on Blake instead. His big eyes. The wrinkled shirt. The waves in his hair, and the freckles on his arms. All of these traits she loved. Perhaps it was selfish, but she didn't want the sick moon to take those things away.

"How long, do you think?"

He shook his head. "We don't know if this is the end, right? Maybe it's just a weird phenomenon."

She could tell he didn't believe his own words. Her thoughts went back to the Instagram comments. One had stuck with her, sewing itself into her memory with vicious stitches.

We should have listened to those scientists. They tried to warn us. Remember that article?

The article on something shifting within the moon hadn't been the only warning. There had been a few different teams of scientists in the spotlight not too long ago. Phycologists from both the freshwater and ocean studies of algae, and geologists, and others Ana couldn't remember the name of. She'd skimmed through the videos and articles, sure, but like so many others, she hadn't dug deep into the warnings.

"I couldn't sleep," Blake said and broke through her spiraling thoughts. "I kept having weird dreams, and then the cat started hissing. The bedroom was glowing. Freaky as hell."

Ana had to laugh. "Typical Walt Whisker, hissing even during the end times."

Blake cracked a smile, too.

"Now what?"

He held out his hand. "Come to bed."

She took up his offer and followed him to the bedroom, where Walt crawled out from under the bed. The cat curled between them and purred with a sense of calm. His green eyes closed in contentment, and the long whiskers twitched. Ana relaxed on her side, trying not to think about the itching beneath her skin, but it felt like a thousand spiders danced there. Even in the horrible green blaze, Blake's face was a comfort.

She'd always associated the color with plants and forests. Soft moss and spring. Life. How could it bring the moon such sickness? Such death?

Blake held her with one arm, giving Walt Whisker enough room to shift and curl between them. "How did all of this happen so quickly?"

Ana scratched the purring feline behind the ears. Stroked his gray and white fur, then had to look away from the small nose and whiskers so her heart wouldn't catch in her throat.

"We'd been warned," she said, going back to her earlier thoughts of the news stories. One in particular covered the fact that over 400,000 pounds of man-made trash littered the moon. Something sprouted from the galactic garbage, the teams had said on the news. Something with life.

Oh. She'd forgotten. The memory came back with a punch, taking the breath from her.

"Algae," she murmured. "Do you remember? They said some perfect leakage of the space trash created an environment for an algae bloom. All it takes is the right condition, and something can sprout. Evolve."

How fast it multiplied, found a way to persevere even in harsh conditions. Once life began, it must have migrated across the moon's surface with stunning speed. Such a strange little organism… Algae had adapted to live on ice, so why not the moon?

Everyone cared for a day, when the algae story first came out. The next day, though, coverage was replaced with shinier and bloodier news across the country.

Ana didn't understand all of the science behind it, and there was little sense in trying to puzzle it out. She could lay here with Blake and Walt Whisker and ask a million questions about why and how, she could cast her wildest theories out into the universe and shout them to the sky above, but come morning, the end result would be the same. Either the planet would sustain, or it would not.

It was more than the destruction of the moon. That dust the algae created, like a plague of lime-tinted pollen, was already changing Earth. Whether it originated from space or dirt hardly seemed to matter. It was here, clinging to the windows and burning her skin. She didn't tell Blake about the itch, about how she wanted to take a hot knife to her arm and cut the flesh away.

"What are you thinking about?" He blinked those big eyes at her.

"We left a graveyard of trash on the moon. Of course something would rise from that, you know? Something learned how to sustain itself."

"Even if that meant taking out all other life with it?"

"I guess we'll never know."

"Yeah," he said, a frown tugging his mouth down. "An explanation would have offered some comfort, I guess."

Ana reached for his hand, entwined their fingers. This was comfort, the feeling of his warm skin against hers.

Walt Whisker sat up, his spine arched and tail fluffed. An agitated *mrrow* filled the quiet home. A second later, windows rattled as the ground trembled. Ana had never felt an earthquake before, but maybe this was something different.

Blake held her close as panic sent her heart into overdrive.

"It's the end of the world, and we're in bed," she whispered into the crook of his neck, breathing in the familiar cologne he had put on earlier in the day.

"I wouldn't want to be anywhere else." He kissed her head, and she shifted back to look him in the eyes again.

The power surged, killing the small lamplight and glow from the clock in the bedroom, which meant the Wi-Fi would be gone, too. Only the eerie luminosity from outside remained to bring light to the room.

"Did you respond to any texts or calls?"

Blake shook his head. "No. My phone was blown up with things I'd missed, but when I woke up, I went to find you first."

"I feel selfish, not answering when I had the chance," she confessed. Maybe she was the same as everyone on those comments she'd read earlier. Giving away their sadness and secrets as the world trembled on the brink of collapse. She doubted the phone would have service now.

"I don't think there's a textbook answer to this situation." Blake kissed her then, and all the terror in the world melted away, if for a mere moment.

Another earthquake. Sirens wailed from the far distance in town, but everything else was so quiet. The algae bloom grew thicker outside, completely obscuring the windows in mossy green. They didn't have neighbors. No one to go check on, or anyone to come check on them.

Walt Whisker settled between them again, his gray tail with white flecks flicking left and right. Ears perked.

Ana caught her breath, willed her heart to calm, and then settled into their old routine. So many nights, before all the hell and haze, they would curl together like this. Walt would purr or meow at something only he could see, and then she'd say…

"Do you think Walt has a poem for us tonight?"

Blake blinked, then grinned at the question. The same question she'd ask any night when she wanted to hear him recite a poem. They did name their cat Walt Whisker in honor of the "Good Gray Poet," after all.

Blake hummed in thought and scooped Walt up closer to them. He leaned toward the purring creature. "Read us a poem, Walt," he said to the cat, as he always did during this game.

And when the next rumble came from outside, the windows shook so hard she was sure they'd break. They held up for now. Was that a small fissure in the window behind Blake, or was her mind playing tricks?

There was barely a breeze, and not even a sound from animals outside. The quiet unsettled her most of all, and she returned her gaze to Blake, waiting for his words to cut the silence away.

"Does he have one about the moon?"

Blake paused for a moment. "Well, I can think of one, but it's not very happy."

"That's okay," she said.

Blake cleared his throat and hid his face behind the cat's head. Walt continued his purring, used to the weirdness of his humans, Ana was sure. She let herself pretend Walt Whisker was reading them a poem, one more time.

"Look down, fair moon and bathe this scene / Pour softly down night's nimbus floods, on faces ghastly, swollen, purple / On the dead, on their backs, with their arms toss'd wide / Pour down your unstinted nimbus, sacred moon."

Ana absorbed the words, picturing too clearly the mentioned faces. "That was an interesting one. I wonder what inspired it? I suppose the moon sees all in a way, life and death, all in the perspective of night."

"Maybe Whitman saw a moon that scared him once, too."

Ana huffed out a laugh. "If we live, I'll write a poem about the algae moon then."

Blake caressed her cheek. They both knew there was no surviving this.

Ana closed her eyes and snuggled closer to him. She imagined herself outside, soaking in the green haze. Letting the algae dust her skin until it grew and bloomed into its strongest form. For a moment, temptation to tread back into the night surged in her thoughts. The itch in her arm grew, crawling up into her shoulders and then her chest. A prickle filled her lungs, making her breath come out in hitched waves.

The burn settled deep, from skull to torso to toe. It clung to something in her very cells, rewiring the atoms inside of her. The notion sounded insane even in her own mind, but she could *feel* it.

"I think it's blooming in me," she muttered, eyes closed. "The germination, it's delicious."

"What?"

"I see it painting my bones green. So many spores, twirling in my blood."

The ground shook once more, and she saw the shift of tectonic plates, too. Fractures opening around the world, inviting foreign dust to settle deep into the Earth's core. Would something new regrow from this, or would the planet simply swallow itself?

"It's okay," Blake whispered. "Shh, it's okay."

Glass shattered. Not in the bedroom, thankfully, but from somewhere downstairs. Even one broken window was bad enough. The bloom reached inside, Ana knew. It would stretch its algae fingers upstairs, then everywhere. All of those gentle cells rising into the air, covering them like a blanket.

"It's beautiful," Ana said and choked out a sob. Tears flowed down, and she opened her eyes. Blake looked back at her with an expression she couldn't believe was for her. An expression of terror. She moved closer, and he flinched. During all of their years together, he had never flinched. Never recoiled.

"Blake?" She gripped his shirt, pulled him toward her. The cat scrambled away, hiding on the other side of Blake and hissing at the air where forest-green spores had come to dance in the emerald glow.

His shaking hand reached up, wiped away the tears on her face. Even in the hazy glimmer of the room, she could tell her tears were thick and green, like muck from a swamp. The liquid from her eyes settled on Blake's finger, and his skin absorbed it with parched enthusiasm.

"It's beautiful," she repeated. Her lips tingled, and she needed Blake near her. Touching her. She kissed him hard, and when she felt him relax into her body, she cried again with the joy of having him here with her.

Ana pulled away from the kiss. She'd left a trail of green dust behind on his quiet lips.

"I'm sorry," she said.

"It's okay," he whispered once again. "We're together, and it'll be okay."

She hoped he meant it.

The bloom skulked up the walls as the house shook once more. Glass splintered from the windows on both sides of the bedroom. Algae floated instead, drifting more like feathers than a solid form, but this was no ordinary organism. Algae birthed from the moon, intelligent and able to spread through hundreds of thousands of miles, from moon to Earth, in minutes.

Extraordinary, she thought. *Beautiful.*

Ana glanced outside through the broken window, and searched through the haze for the moon. No more silver shine, but the full moon still smoldered with radiant green. The streaks of red and brown, even black algae, made themselves more apparent than she'd seen earlier in those photos. It all swirled together from moon to Earth, space to soil. A communication she could only ever hope to understand.

Glass shards cut her feet, but she barely felt it, too transfixed on the universe changing before her eyes. Blake's left hand entwined with hers. In his right arm, he held Walt Whisker, who was stained green but otherwise meowed and stayed curled against Blake's side.

Ana turned toward her husband, beaming as he looked at her. His jade-tinted lips met hers. He pulled away, and the glow beneath his pores grew stronger, bioluminescent. Pleasant spores fluttered in her belly when he squeezed her hand.

Blake closed his eyes. Ana knew what he would see there, just as she had—a universe evolving into viridescence.

He smiled. "It's beautiful."

AS HUMANS BURN BENEATH US

We should have been endless. An unlimited inspiration for humans to look up at, to trace invisible patterns around our billowing puffs of particles and name us dragons, or castles, or whatever wonder their imagination created. It's a shame the creativity of humans could not extend to saving their own planet. We thought we'd be forever in this sky, but to condemn our remaining network to Earth is to condemn the last of us to an irreversible death.

Below us, a small human boy in a turquoise shirt glances up. Waves a frantic hand. He names us cotton candy, though we are no such thing.

Perhaps he's not too far off. The spectacular orange-sorbet sky bleeds into raspberry sunset. This will be one of the last nights when our wispy bodies pull and stretch like dark purple taffy across dusk's dazzling colors.

We are dying. When the first of us vanished, the humans barely noticed. When they did notice, oblivious human lips twisted to name it "normal," and we wonder what has happened in their great brains to think such things could ever be normal.

We do not think of humanity as stupid, yet with all of their evolved creations and technology, their collective selfishness never could come together wholly enough to solve the mystery of our disappearances.

Now that the first clouds have gone, the rest will follow rapidly. Awareness weighs heaviest in our vapors, with knowledge of our impending termination. Unlike the humans, however, we can cling to hope. We can set aside one droplet, hide it like the cherished prize the humans could never see it to be, and generate clouds again when humanity destroys itself.

Turquoise Shirt walks into a house with protective panels and strange tubes that snake around from ground to bricks, ideas humans cobbled together to help keep their bodies cool. So much they have normalized, yet there is so much gone.

Do they understand what will happen when the last of us vanishes? All of their science at hand, and all they've done is create Pandora's box, let the lid of the sky crack open, then act surprised at what sprung forth from that burning chasm. They will never be prepared for what emerges, even though the fault remains their own. The most imaginative of dystopian fantasies could never come close to the searing pain of their inevitable demise, of their skin bubbling before fleshy chunks liquefy and slide off bones like thickly oiled globs. So many will watch their children die first, and even that thought has never been enough to propel humanity into significant changes.

They hardly notice our loss, but we notice their chaos, and when the last human falls to their knees, shins sticking to lava-like asphalt on buckled pavement, when their organs wither to dried prunes and tumbleweed lungs, we will rejoice. Even if we're gone, we will find joy somehow through the extinction of humankind.

Water will find a way, and every droplet will learn when to stop its evolution. Transformation back into plants, into rivers, into panthers and shining green beetles, but never back into the two-legged walkers who destroy everything when it does not hurry up for them, when it does not match their schedule. Did the humans schedule themselves to die?

If not, they should. We want to watch as many as we can burn before the last of us evaporates. Our collective memory from the beginning of time until the almost-end will store every sweet drop of human suffering.

Unbearable humidity overwhelms the outdoors. Those lucky enough to have air conditioning in their homes will learn to adapt or die, because everything will soon break. No new clouds are poised to form. We are done. With nowhere to go, water hangs heavy in the air, slickens the skin of all those who dare step outside, away from their protective indoor sanctuaries.

It only takes one degree. One small degree of Earth warming up, and listen, do they hear it? Flight turbulence disturbs machines in the air, the protection of clouds long gone, so where does the sunlight bounce? Nowhere. Hot air rises in uneven eruptions, shaking once smooth flights into bad ones; most of the planes manage to land, others fall from the sky. Comets burning through the horizon so fast, so hot. Nothing left of the plane's body, or the human bodies. When sun rises and the last newscasters aim to cover such tragedies, there will be nothing left for cameras to capture, assuming the equipment can withstand the heat.

Some humans are smart, stocked up on water and supplies, but no level of preparedness can save them from what's to come. How could they ever prepare for the lessening of rain, for no more snow, for water sources to dry into brittle beds of sawdust and heartbreak?

The ones who survive longest will be the ones who have the most water, until others with guns arrive to shoot away those smart brains that thought to hide precious supplies. No more water, no more brains. Meanwhile, others in private rockets will fly away to space, laugh. Rejoice at the promise of a new colony. Humans will do what they do best: Consume. Take until nothing remains, watch their own uncles and dogs and mothers crumple into dead, dry spiders.

In another part of the world, as Turquoise Shirt gets ready for sleep, another child wakes up, sunlight peeks through her window, glistens in harsh brightness against desert sand outside her family's home. Dust grains mix with water vapor. Air condenses. Cloud droplets form, rise to join us far above the town, but this process is in danger. Everything here a hazard, and the humans should have spelled out W A R N I N G in the sky with neon paint, flown the message across their shriveling planet about the disappearance of clouds, but we are too insignificant for them to recognize as important. As essential. As the monster who will let them burn.

We do not feel pity. Not anymore. What follows could only ever be a consequence of their own inaction.

Beyond the desert, something terrible detonates. The little boy will wake up, watch the news with his parents just before static takes over the television. Similar white noise will rule radio stations and infect human minds with terror because our departure mixed with the Molotov medley of a tragic accident is destined to send the climate spiraling into its already irreversible trajectory.

What happens next makes Chernobyl look laughable.

The governments call it an accident, and we wonder if the humans believe them this time, as they always have. Or maybe they'll realize the powerful have grown tired of waiting for Earth's demise, see how ready the elite are to jet their own worthy people away to a space settlement, where the majority of human populace is not invited.

No clouds here in the desert. We've scattered. Why has so much radioactive waste and new material been stored in such a dry area without other humans noticing? Their ignorant faith in higher powers, in government figures, baffles us.

Clouds hover no more. Nothing left to absorb outgoing radiation. Without the clouds, no barrier exists to diminish the blow, to lessen the way energy travels between space and Earth. Only warmth, a kind of blue-flame heat that ricochets up from a mushroom cloud of toxic chemicals lit aflame, will be all the humans know as they suffocate on air thick with burning ash.

We leave. Our remnants gather far away from the false cloud of the desert. The only cloud there now. A horrid plume consisting of ammonia-scented toxic waste before it mingles with odors of flesh melting off faces. Finger bones char to glowing embers. Clothes disintegrate. The girl in the desert exists no more. Her skin reduced to sticky stretches of bubblegum meat, connecting her upper body to the clay wall of her family's home. Miraculously, the wall stands. The girl's remains dangle from it, slumped forward, melted to its surface.

Eternal, we once filled the sky with stratus, with cirrus thin as willows and blooming kernels of popcorn puffs, forming shapes for the humans to assign us silly names. No more.

No more cooling. Sunlight is not softened. Instead, it meets nuclear blasts and radioactive plumes, and fries the boy in the turquoise shirt like a sticky egg to the sidewalk before his parents find him, scream their heads off as their own heat demise arrives. Liquefies skeletons to seep between cement cracks down into Earth's roots, its breaking crust, its cracking core.

We once stretched miles across the whole planet, and now we're scarce. Near extinct. Lightweight vapors woven into something great, suspended like magic disguised in complicated physics. The humans did not protect us. They did not save the dolphins or polar bears. They did not care when rainforests burnt to cinders and deforestation prevailed. Ignorant eyes win devastating prizes.

We don't mean to be callous clouds, but the humans took sick glee in prepping their doomsdays and playing make-believe apocalypse. Yet when wildfires seized land and tornadoes swallowed towns, when foolish spills turned clear waters black, what did humanity do?

All dead. All gone. We're almost gone, too. A handful remains. Connected to all of us through wispy tendrils, we hold onto the last clouds. Watch together as it all ends. If we were to fall to Earth instead of having been forced to disappear, we would have fallen so gently, a patchy white veil of vapor leaving thin watery sheens on surfaces… No harm. No death.

Instead, we did not fall. We vanish.

Climatologists cautioned what would happen if Earth warmed one degree, two degrees… And now the coral reefs are bleached-out specks of dust, fish are nothing but rotting carcasses, the planet ravaged by both flood and drought, by drowning and flames, nothing cancels each other out when the whole system shatters. Even the liquid of blood congeals into hard putty within seconds.

Two degrees turns to four degrees of warming.

One cloud remains, a threadbare wisp of a thing barely able to store the death of Earth in our spiderweb-thin vein of memory. Boy in turquoise shirt and girl in desert have been dead long enough for their bones to morph into dust, because that is the kind of heat humans have created and assumed the planet would be just fine.

Massive loss of species. If any insects or animals survive, even we cannot see them from the sky. They will not last much longer. Remaining humans have hunkered down into bunkers, deep below dirt, seeking coolness, but so little can be found. Weather obeys no master now, and it will destroy them all one way or another.

Savage meteorological conditions reign—dry storms learned to create something akin to lightning without rain or wind or clouds. We have never seen fiery bolts like these, and even we are unsure of what to call such terror. Spears of flame pierce through cracked sky and strike down onto chalky terrain.

No one can adapt to this.

Eight-degree warming follows and brings with it an unimaginable destruction. We were never supposed to let change spiral this large, clouds and humans alike, all of life, this was not the plan. Not now, so soon. Not ever.

The final change ruptures Earth's heart apart. One last lightning strike fractures the sky, splits crust and mantle as if it has gripped a supercontinent in invisible hands and splintered it apart. We were here for Pangea, and we are almost here for the end as flames spew from the deepest grotto beneath cores and engulf everything in one last bright orange-sorbet light, how it soars across the falling sky, eerie but similar to a last pretty sunset where a boy in a turquoise shirt still dreamed. The naked atmosphere shudders, and bolts of fire from that strange dry lightning glow with unnatural colors.

Whatever it is, it has evolved.

The last cloud we see before we die is a familiar radioactive billow, something that exists outside of our network. Something we cannot communicate with.

Nuclear lightning descends upon the traumatized planet. Perhaps one day it will seek out a place for us, but until then, what such change creates after the last cloud disappears, we will never know.

THE BONES HE PLANTED

Plumes of gray clouds drifted across early afternoon sky and momentarily blocked out the sun. The rain held off, for which Dahl remained thankful. He knew Terra was at home digging, digging, digging…

She should wait for me to get back.

If something happened to her while he was away, he'd never forgive himself.

One more client to deal with today, and then he'd risk a speeding ticket to get home. Still, a nagging voice vibrated in his thoughts, pushing paranoia to the forefront until he dialed their landline. Terra hated cellphones.

Each ring sent a sticky vine of worry to root deeper inside his brain.

"Hi, hon," Terra's voice cut through the static.

Relief sighed its way through his tense body. "Hey green-thumb, how goes the dirt battle?"

She laughed and it was music. He saw it often, the heaving effort it sometimes took for her weary muscles to produce a laugh or a smile. Even sneezes sent wracks of pain throughout her body.

"Not bad," she said through a stifled yawn. "Almost

done digging. Taking a rest before I finish. Better to get it in the dirt as soon as possible."

"Delivery went okay?"

"Mhmm. The delivery kid took off like a spooked dog. I guess this one came from a mutated batch. Whatever that means."

"I thought they were mutated to begin with?"

She huffed out a short laugh. "I like to think of them as cosmic more than mutated. The dealer said the soil was different this time, too much of an ingredient, but it should be fine."

"If you say so."

She chuckled again, a melody he'd secretly recorded one evening on his phone. Desperation drove him to preserve that sound, before their house became filled with inevitable silence.

Dahl didn't understand much about these trees. It all sounded like pseudoscience. A damned tree, even if it was grown in the most precious minerals on Earth and from space alike, wasn't going to cure what had taken up sticky residence inside of Terra.

She'd explained some of it before—well, she had tried. Whereas her brain bloomed in thoughts like rose petals, recollected the past with whispering reeds and forest-green tendrils, Dahl's mind buzzed with simple wires connecting A to B. Occasionally, creativity sparked there, but it was never anything like how Terra could take a tiny seedling idea and turn it into a lush garden.

During the days when she couldn't work outside, Terra had been curled on the couch with her laptop, and Dahl watched her sink deeper into a forum of other people who were sick. Chatting with others who understood seemed to bring her comfort, but then she found a group who claimed to be cured. Dahl had done his best not to scoff at the discussions held there, at least not in front of Terra. The forum members followed a dendrologist with cult-like worship, and claimed his trained growers, who sounded more like alchemists, grew trees that could cure ailments, even ones as deadly as Terra's illness.

The dendrologist had access to a powerful pulverizer that ground meteorites to dust, which was then mixed with a curated soil for his trees to grow in. What the hell could meteorite dirt accomplish that the medical world couldn't? Dahl never received an answer.

Money-thieving snakes obsessed with cosmic dust… The particles could have been bits of plastic for all any of them knew. Profiting off of sickness and desperation, how could it end well? But Terra wanted to try, and he wasn't so much of a bastard that he'd say no to his dying wife.

"I don't think it's a magical cure, Dahl," she said. "I just want to leave something behind. Some kind of life that you can watch grow in our yard and remember me."

"You know I don't need that to remember you."

"But this tree will be special." She coughed, paused. A heavy sigh pushed its way through the connection. "The grower was anxious to get rid of this one, actually. Tried to sell me three of them for dirt cheap." Her voice caught again, and Dahl listened as she struggled to regulate her breathing. Exhaustion slithered its way so easily into her body.

"I'll be home in about two hours. Just have to help a guy with a malware issue down on Lues Street. I can help you with the rest." He flipped his turn signal on and checked the GPS—only ten minutes away from the customer's house.

Terra inhaled, her sharp resolve sounding clearly through the phone. "No. After this, I don't think I'll be strong enough for any more gardening. This is the last one I'll get to do alone. I have to plant it."

The diagnosis had been long and grim. She would die, Dahl knew. He had repeated those words to himself many times, but the reality refused to settle in his fogged mind. Life without Terra hardly seemed like a life. She was his reality, his home. They always found comfort in each other.

She refused chemo, and he wanted to support her, but some twisted part of his grieving mind insisted she was choosing death. It was a ridiculous thought, as if she even had a choice in how she'd leave him behind. The cancer spreading like parasitic tar inside her body would take her no matter what, and she wanted to be as much of herself as possible before that day's shrouded arrival.

A miracle, Dahl wished and even prayed for. He'd never been a religious man, but desperate people searched for desperate hope.

"Will it grow, do you think? Will it survive?" he asked, knowing little about what she had brought into their garden. Her beloved botanical paradise.

"It better. Certainly isn't the most welcoming thing to see in someone's yard, but maybe that will be good for us." Her wicked humor, it never left her. Neither of them cared much for visitors.

"Well, you rest for as long as you need to. Love you, and I'll see you soon."

"You got it, hon. I love you."

Dahl said goodbye and concentrated on the row of faded houses down Lues Street. The doctor told them Terra's "good" days were limited. But she held her head high between the fatigue, the sickness, the days she could not eat and the days when her breathing came in rough, ragged gulps.

A hard lump formed in Dahl's throat. The client's house waited in front of his parked vehicle; the chipped silver paint on the siding gleamed in the sun like something sterile. Colorful, swaying blooms of early summer danced in the breeze alongside the overgrown foliage by the fence. He rubbed his hands against his face as if he could push the pain back into the cavern of his skull.

Darker clouds amassed overhead as Dahl pulled into his driveway. The sweet yet sharp aroma of mint and lavender greeted him from their front porch where Terra's potted plants soaked in the sun.

Inside the house, late afternoon light stretched through the big windows in the living room, tinting the white carpet and bookshelves a burnt orange. A pile of blankets told him Terra had chosen to rest in the reading nook, which the sun kept toasty throughout the afternoon. Like a cat seeking warmth, she had nestled into the spot. Dahl's chest ached as he approached and caught a glimpse of her gaunt form. A mound of blankets covered her body. Dark, tousled hair streaked with her first few strands of gray fanned out around her on a small pillow.

Love pooled heavy in his heart. He wished he could reach inside her and remove the cancer the way he removed malware and viruses from computers. But the inner wiring and network of the human body eluded him. Nothing about this situation would ever come to an understanding inside his anguished thoughts. He leaned down to gently brush the hair away from her face.

Cold skin grazed his fingertips. Beneath the strands of hair, Terra's cheek appeared stiff and pale.

"Terra?" his choked whisper of a voice called out to her. Carefully, he placed a hand beneath her chin and moved her head toward him. Her jaw jutted forward, loose, and fell open slightly. All tension was erased from her bloodless face—a face no longer her own, but one created by cancer's uninvited and relentless carving.

A damp spot soaked through the lower half of the blankets, assaulting his senses with its sharp odor.

Death was an ugly thing in its reality, and although nothing about Terra could ever repulse him, Dahl stumbled away from the body. His foot snagged the coffee table and he landed hard on the floor. Wracking sobs punched his lungs and throat as he cried out into the nothingness. Alone.

He crawled back toward Terra and wrapped his arms around her, nearly pulling her to the floor with him.

"You were supposed to wait for me. You were supposed to wait…" His voice was lost beneath animal howls of sorrow; a horrible screeching ripped its way from his throat and shredded his vocal cords until he no longer recognized the cries as his own.

Pain morphed time into a blur. When he finally loosened his stranglehold on the body and tucked the blankets back in around her, he stood up and glanced around the darkened room in a brief bout of robotic clarity.

He should call the coroner, or the ambulance? How does that work? *What do I do first?*

Maybe he should call Terra's parents.

Maybe he should strap her into his car and drive himself off that big bridge in the city where they were still doing construction. The name of the bridge…he couldn't remember. He drove past it every day on the way to his office.

Laughter bubbled from his throat. Manic and echoing in the dark. Terra was dead, and here he was trying to remember the name of a goddamned bridge. He laughed until an icy, choking sensation gripped his lungs and he fell to his knees on the floor, gasping for breath. Another bout of uncontrolled wailing loomed, dwelled within his heart and gut, but *no, no I don't have the energy. Not again. Terra…*

He inhaled. Exhaled. Fought down the roiling nausea in his stomach. Looked up and for the first time spotted it in the middle of the kitchen across from the living room. Had it been there the whole time?

Dahl forced himself to stand and stumble over to the kitchen. He flipped the light on. The swollen-thorn sapling stood silent in the kitchen's glow. It was a young tree, only about three feet tall, but the prominent bullhorn shape of thickening thorns poked out from short twigs. Feathery fronds with an eggplant hue clung around the thorns. Above the leaves were tiny, green doughnut-like circles that emitted a sweet, nectar scent.

A card tied to the sapling's trunk read: *Vachellia cornigera—Bullhorn Acacia. Dear owner, this acacia is the one you requested, but it is abnormal. Malum. I would have destroyed it, but it would not let me. Give it only death, not life.*

Dahl read the card three times. *Malum…* Evil? How could a tree be evil? Terra had searched for the perfect tree from online sellers in the states, since importing it from Mexico or Central America would have taken more time than she knew she had left. The Bullhorn Acacia itself was known for being strange, for its ability to create a strong and addictive symbiotic relationship between the ants it provided nectar to. Protection for sustenance. Terra had imagined something romantic about it, but then this one, she said, this one from the dendrologist in California had been different.

She had mentioned something about mutated genes, but Dahl had no idea what it meant. He just nodded along and helped her order it. A final gift to his green-thumb girl, his sweet wife…

Dead now. Dead.

Give it only death, not life.

How do you give something death? *Death has been given to me,* he thought. *Maybe I have to give it back.*

Dahl stared at the blinking message on the landline phone, most likely from Terra's family. Had they called at the same time she'd taken her last breath? They needed to know she was gone. That the cancer had taken away their greatest light. Cancer. Evil. *Malum.*

A shiver pinched at Dahl's neck as he walked over to the sapling. His mind seemed to detach slightly from his reality as he picked up the tree with its base in a container. He watched Terra plant so many things, but he prayed to any existing higher power that he didn't fuck this one up.

Give it only death. But she wanted to give it life. With her dying breath, she wished to plant this thing in the soil and have it grow, a reminder of her for Dahl to watch and take care of, always. A final gift.

The dominion of death, its terrible and black shroud, seemed to absorb Dahl totally as he stepped into the night on the back deck. He felt around for the light switch and flooded the yard with an artificial glow. Thankful their closest neighbors were three miles away, he went to work.

The area Terra had started digging needed to be deeper. Her tools remained on the ground, lying beside a dirt pile. He ignored the twinge in his chest and dug, sloping the sides and making sure the hole was deeper than the tree's container. And then he continued, digging lower, wider, until the hole morphed into a rectangle. Big enough to fit a shallow coffin. Sweat clung to him in the heated night and gnats stuck to his skin. Mosquitoes left behind itchy bites, but still he persisted.

The soil in the acacia's container was moist, and the root ball did not put up a fight when he removed it. Most of the roots were intact, but he struggled to untangle a snarled circle. With Terra's pruners, he aimed to cut through the hopeless mass. He moved toward the root, but something held him there, an invisible force impeding direct contact with the blade. The strain shook his body with an aching weight as he grumbled and tried to push back against the thing he could not see. The pressure gave way, and the pruners slid forward, slicing a clean line across the side of his unprotected hand.

"Damn!" A stinging heat burst through his flesh, and blood dripped down to the soil. When he tried again, the pressure disappeared. Blades cleanly cut through the matted root. Unable to trust his own mind, he ignored the phantom presence and continued. For Terra.

He went inside to get her, the pruners still clutched in his hand. She needed to see what he was creating for her.

"Time to get up, hon." He stroked her cheek and kissed her chilled forehead. With careful hands, he removed what he could of the soiled clothes, and then used the pruners to cut away at the rest of the dampened fabric. A reddish-purple hue colored her sides and the back of her legs. The once strong and full body turned skeletal beneath cancer's dark spell.

Dahl filled a big plastic bowl with water and brought over a sponge and soap to get her cleaned up. He steadied his hands and let his mind drift. Memories looped through a reel of their honeymoon in Italy. Her dark-humored jokes. The emerald green dress she wore on their fifteenth anniversary. If love could bring her back, surely his love would have burst by now and spilled itself out like a bleeding sacrifice to the reaper.

Silent tears found their way into his eyes again like damp pinpricks. He let them fall while he deposited the bowl in the kitchen sink and rinsed out the muck. The dirt. *All dirt in the end, all of us.* We belonged to nature, he knew. Terra understood that better than most.

Her muscles had stiffened, but he lifted her into his arms and tried not to focus on the heavy, cold flesh. The emptiness of it. How her eyelids had crept open.

Back into the night's encirclement, he tenderly set Terra down inside the bed of upturned earth. The deck lights provided him with enough illumination to work with, but the night was warm and hazy, and time still felt blurry. Unreal. Like this was another dimension of reality altogether.

He reached for the pruners and ignored the hot pulsation from the slash against his skin.

"I'm sorry about this part, Terra," he murmured. She'd understand.

The pruners were new, sharp, with scissoring blades that punctured well into her skin, but left jagged marks from his shaking hands. He navigated around the bones and concentrated on her belly, slicing through epidermis and hardened muscles, choking on the fetid stench that erupted from the pierced liver and stomach. Liquid and goop, strings of meat, it all seeped from her body and appeared black in the dimmed light. His hands plunged inside the opened cavity of her gut, and he grabbed hold of anything that released itself and came away with his grip.

He removed all he could and let it settle into the soil, moistening earth for the new plant. The wind brought a sweet rustle among the backyard trees, as if they were singing a soothing melody to calm Dahl, to encourage him to finish his project.

He packed soil from above the makeshift grave into his wife's opened and emptied midriff. Carefully, he picked up the base of the acacia and planted the root ball within Terra, below her ribs. He kept a cautious hold of the young tree with one hand, minding its thorns, until the basin of plain dirt was secure enough to hold the rest up. It took another few hours for him to fill in the grave and cover Terra. With each shovel of dirt, he channeled all his love for her into the soil, hoping the strong emotions would transfer into the terrain and cover her like a warm blanket. He created the watering basin, secured everything the best he could, and then let himself wander inside, shower, and fall into a dark, dreamless sleep.

The first month was not the worst. Terra's parents lived far away, and he deflected their calls by telling them Terra was resting or too sick to talk. The tactic worked initially, but now they wished to come visit, even if it was to say goodbye to their daughter. They both hated flying, and Terra's father was barely recovered from a minor stroke two months prior, but they'd board the plane and fly for her.

"Next month. Maybe next month," he had told them, but next month was here. He ignored their latest call and went to check on the acacia.

The speed with which it grew terrified him. Trees took years to properly grow and thrive, but this particular species, whatever it was, shot up another three feet from when it'd been planted. Thorns thickened, taking on more of the bullhorn shape. Strange leaves almost like ferns sprouted from ends of thin branches and even from the middle of the steer-like thorns. The feathered, purple leaves he'd noticed earlier expanded, as did the green glands that produced nectar. The trunk shape morphed, skeletal at first, but then its middle protruded on two sides, like rib bones. Two branches jutted off in perfect parallelism with thorns curving off like hoofed hands. Throughout the entire tree, trunk and branches, leaves and flowers, ran a faint blue system that connected together all the way into the earth below. The lines shimmered like glittering veins.

Terra surrounded him. Her voice was the wind, and her heart beat on beneath the soil-grave. He wished the acacia's thorns weren't sharp so he could wrap his arms around the tree, see if the bark felt as smooth as it looked, as smooth as Terra had been when she was healthy, when she'd unpeel her clothes and curl into his embrace.

"I have a client in Texas," he told the tree. "Big mess of spyware, but they go through our company, so I have to deal with it." Tentatively, he reached out a hand and stroked the spine of a large thorn. Dark burgundy ants that'd recently swarmed to the tree marched forward but ignored him when he retreated his fingers away. With teeth he could not see, they chewed holes in the thorns and disappeared inside.

"I love you, Terra. I'll be back in a week."

His eyes again hovered over the angry colony of ants traveling across the stems and leaves, security guards over the acacia's life. In return for their protective roles, where they chomped off any threatening vines and bugs, the tree provided a nectar within the leaf stalk so tempting that the ants would kill for it. A deadly and harmonious agreement.

As he turned to leave, the corner of his vision caught a cricket landing on the tree's thin branch. Before the bigger bug hopped away, the colony swarmed and gnawed. A small hind leg fell away and the cricket swayed to the ground, left for the birds or another creature.

The cricket would sing no more songs to the night.

Give it only death.

When Dahl returned from the work trip on Tuesday, he came home to seventeen missed calls and six voice messages on their home phone, all from Terra's parents. The latest one, left yesterday, informed him that they bought plane tickets and would be flying out Friday. Three days from now.

Hot panic swelled in his chest like a lava-filled balloon.

"No, no." He pounded a fist against the counter and tore the landline from its plug in the wall.

Terra. Could he move her? Replant her elsewhere? It was too risky.

He could not kill her again.

Outside, early evening sun splattered gold and pink hues across the summer sky. Lilac clouds drifted lazily, and the scent from the mint plants fragranced the air. The acacia loomed, easily towering over Dahl's six-foot frame. It was impossible for something to grow so quickly, but there it stood. The trunk had widened. Beneath the bark that protruded like ribs, the lower part curved and sloped downward. Branches thickened, as did its thorns. A gnarled circle formed near the top, where lumps jutted out like brow bones and lopsided ears. Dark fuzz pooled in random spots over the bark, emitting the stench of something sickly sweet that barely covered the odor of rot below.

Still, Dahl could see Terra beneath the horror. The way the acacia stood strong, the width of its body, the hollowed slopes where her cheekbones would be.

A tuft of russet-red fur stuck to the bullhorn thorns of the tree—short hairs waved gently along with the breeze. Dahl stepped closer and peered at the fur, bushy and coarse. Something must have gotten trapped in the thorns. A squirrel? Maybe even a fox.

Droplets of blood, dried and dark, stuck to stems and thorns. Ants scurried back and forth, paying the fur no mind. Dahl reached forward to grab the red pelt. The ants stopped their daily marching and scurried toward him as one programmed unit. He retreated before their bites could gnaw a finger off like they did to the cricket's leg.

"Terra," Dahl choked out between gasps of fear. "Your parents are coming in three days, and I don't know what to do." Failure raked down his spine like scratches of heated, sharpened coal. He flinched as pain struck him deeper, and he dove out of the way of the swinging stem with the acacia's thorns.

"I'm sorry! I'll find a way to fix it." He would. He'd do anything for her, and she knew that.

Daaahhl, the tree sighed. From somewhere beneath its base, from somewhere deep in the soil where she was buried, Terra whispered to him.

"I'll make it right, my green-thumb girl. I'll make it right again."

Give it only death. Malum.

On Wednesday, the tree caught a rabbit. The piercing scream of an injured animal jolted Dahl awake from where he'd fallen asleep in the reading nook. He dreamed he had died there too, that his body melted into Terra's ghost imprinted on the blankets.

In a daze, he bolted toward the horrible shriek and scrambled out onto the deck. The small, brown body was desperately trying to yank itself away from where the ants surrounded it, trapping the cotton-tailed creature against thorns as they gathered. The savage protectors swarmed and bit at the rabbit's hind leg.

The cry was one of the worst things Dahl had ever heard. It rang inside his head as if he'd swallowed a screeching fire alarm. The break in his heart felt tangible. He opened his mouth and screamed for the innocent animal as he thrust his hand between the stems and batted the ants away.

Their bites pierced into his flesh like stinging needles of fire; his hand went numb in seconds from whatever poison they carried, whatever the tree gave to them. Nothing normal resided within this monster disguised as nature, within these ants or the nectar they killed for. He swung his arm and his numb hand toward the rabbit, freeing the creature of its entrapment by the thorns, and then used his other hand to carefully avoid the ants and grab the rabbit by the scruff, pulling it away as it screamed and bled onto the branches until he stumbled away from the tree and collapsed on the ground.

He held the rabbit and wept as it wriggled in his grasp, its chest heaving in panic—the back leg a crimson mess with patches of skin showing between matted fur. It calmed for just a moment, and Dahl met the hare's dark eyes.

Malum, the stare seemed to accuse. *Why did you bring this thing here?*

The rabbit twisted again and darted crookedly toward the far undergrowth by the gap in the fence. A trail of bloody prints stained the grass.

"She's lonely," he whispered to himself, to the acacia, to anything that'd listen. And then he looked at the tree. "You can't kill things because you're lonely."

Whhhy not? it whispered back. *Hhhumans do it all the time.*

"Are you not human, Terra?"

Silence.

Thursday. Her parents would arrive tomorrow, and Dahl had nothing to tell them. Nothing to show except a wicked tree in the backyard that he named Terra. As if naming something could grant him power over it.

Yes here, you see, this is your daughter now, come look, come love her from afar. We can't hug her, but the cancer is gone. The cancer is gone.

He picked up the pruners from the kitchen table and stuck them in his back pocket before walking outside to talk to her once again. To understand a question he could not quite form on his tongue.

Dahhhl.

He closed his eyes and remembered the card tied to the sapling's trunk before it sprouted into whatever this was. *Vachellia cornigera—Bullhorn Acacia. Malum.*

Evil.

Terra could never be evil. "I'm so sorry," he whispered into the tree's stems. He caressed the thorns with careful hands and avoided the ants. No more blood.

He could give no more blood to the tree. He had wanted to give Terra one last beautiful thing, to plant the tree she'd been fascinated by, to grow something with her that would outlive them both. If it had been beautiful, maybe he could've told her parents, shown them the splendor of Terra's smooth bark and blossoming leaves, but her true self was lost beneath the terror-stricken reign of the thing growing and growing in his backyard.

Come to me, Dahhhl.

"Sorry, sorry. So sorry."

Hhhold me.

"No more death, Terra. If your parents come tomorrow, I have no lies to tell them. I'd only be able to show them your tree."

Let them come. The ants frenzied around the stems, as if excited for the chance to spill more blood, to let it rain upon the thorns. Dahl wondered if blood was in the nectar the acacia had been feeding them.

"You deserved more life than the world gave you. I only made you worse, more ruined than the cancer ever could have. Only gave you pain."

Come to me now.

One step forward, his heart heavy. His back pocket weighted with the pruners. Gray clouds formed overhead, dark with the threat of summer storms.

"Why didn't you wait for me to come home?"

The breeze picked up, blowing the stony scent of an oncoming rainfall toward him. He reached for the pruners and held them limp in his hand.

You won't hhhurt me.

"Never." He walked forward, and soil clung to his bare toes. The ants paused and watched, waiting. Tears fell in fat drops and clung to his eyelashes, as if wishing to climb back into his eye sockets and never leave because it was better in there, dark and damp and warm. Out here in the light, pain was exposed, planted between unavoidable scenes.

Curved thorns embraced him. He cried out and plunged the pruners into the heart of the tree, the heart of Terra. A place the cancer never touched completely. The acacia pierced his flesh in return, and the ants hoarded over his body, biting so deep they created craters in his skin and buried themselves inside, but chewing him up from the outside in wouldn't stop the acacia's death.

The tree unlatched a wooden jaw from its center and screamed, and so did Terra from her bed of dirt, and Dahl screamed with them both as the rain fell and drowned him beneath warm drops that mingled with spilled gore.

Black discharge oozed from beneath the pruners still embedded in the acacia. Stuck—his blood, and the pus from a mutated tree. They merged, and he remembered their last phone call and what Terra had said about the acacia. *Certainly isn't the most welcoming thing to see in someone's yard, but maybe that will be good for us....*

He laughed. *Good for us. Get in the dirt quickly now, plant us.*

Together, death and life merged. He'd given the acacia both.

Together, man and nature bled.

A HAUNTING OF LAWN ORNAMENTS

The garden gnomes are the first to contact the underworld.

"They're so creepy," Daisy says as she peers outside our bedroom window.

From here, we have a clear view of the neighbor's garden. The McManns and their yard seemed so normal, but then again, we'd moved into our house during the winter. The little cul-de-sac rounded out into four homes, including ours, and then looped back to Oleander Drive, where more houses stood with their beige or eggshell siding and perfectly landscaped lawns.

During those snowy months, we kept to ourselves, but would wave to fellow neighbors, and we became friendly with the older couple who lived on our right. June and Freddy—they were both in their seventies, very sweet, and had waged an impressive war against our HOA. With a fence painted in tie-dye and matching psychedelic window shutters, their home glowed with notions of peace and free love. June claimed they'd lived there long before the surrounding development was bought, and they had once owned the land where our house now stood. They bargained to sell the lot for twice its worth and only if they could keep their retro rainbow of colors displayed. The homeowner association caved since the developer wanted to complete the lot, so I admired June and Freddy for telling them all to eat rocks.

The couple made Daisy smile, so I liked them even more. Plus, their home felt safe to live next to against the other formulaic Stepford houses.

Our neighbors to the left, however, made no one smile. The McManns emitted a cold standoffishness that was fine until Daisy and I were hauling the last bits of our furniture inside. Mr. McMann introduced himself as Mr. McMann, which sent the first red flag waving in my tired brain. I still don't know his first name.

We'd wanted to get our furniture inside and clean up the salt and slush that had tracked its way in with us, blemishing those new hardwood floors. Mrs. McMann came marching up beside him and asked who was moving into this fine home. No men in sight must have set off some alarm bell in their tiny minds.

"So," Mrs. McMann had said, a permanent scowl etched between her eyes. Her overly processed blonde hair screamed for conditioner. The poorly attached extensions weren't helping. For a second, I contemplated asking which salon she visited so I could make sure we avoided it.

"Which of you two ladies is moving in?" she continued.

"Both of us," Daisy replied, and her wide smile beamed bright like the fresh snow.

"Where are your husbands?"

I laughed in Mrs. McMann's face while Daisy continued to grin, as if she could eat away their arrogance. "I can be the husband today."

Mrs. McMann did not seem to appreciate my wink and humor. I sighed and tried again.

"I'm Brooke. This is my wife, Daisy. We'll be your new neighbors!" Maybe false optimism was the way?

"Oh," Mrs. McMann said. "I thought maybe you were sisters."

This time Daisy laughed. My favorite laugh. The one with a kind of snort you're supposed to save for loved ones and friends, not polite society. We'd been mistaken for a lot of things—good friends, roommates, co-workers sharing an apartment . . . But sisters, well that was a first, given our different complexions and eye color. Her curly hair and my half-shaven stick-straight strands. Adopted sisters looked more alike. The only similar trait we shared were our matching wedding bands.

Daisy cleared her throat, and I could tell she was fighting the urge to laugh again. "Well, nice meeting you." She grabbed a box marked "kitchen" and shoved past these two fools, since they'd decided to stand right on the path leading up to our front door. Did they expect us to trudge in the snow-covered yard around them?

Probably.

That was the end of getting to know the McManns. At least through conversation. Once we learned we could spy on their yard through our bedroom blinds, we couldn't help it. Every Monday morning, Mr. McMann lumbered out to their upstairs balcony—an additional feature to these homes that must have cost them a pretty penny. He stared at the small woods behind the cul-de-sac. Just stood and stared. No sipping of coffee, no muttering to himself. Only silence, for a solid ten minutes.

"What do you think he's doing?" Daisy had asked when we caught him doing this for the fourth morning in a row.

"Maybe he wants some alone time while the kids get ready for school?"

"I don't know," she said.

"Maybe he's waiting for something to happen. An alarm call to pick up arms and storm the gates!"

"Shut up," Daisy said playfully. "He seems too soft for that."

We rarely saw Mrs. McMann until she emerged from the front door, hair curled, plush coat, some expensive boots beneath tailored trousers. She looked ready to take on the world in those outfits, I admit. Instead, she'd walk the kids down to the curb where the school bus stopped, then she returned inside until later in the afternoon when the kids came home.

The kids. They're the interesting ones. And maybe the ones who led to the gnomes summoning a demonic entity.

The three McMann children bear the tragic names of Kayleigha and McKarty for the girls, and something like Titan Jexson for the boy. You know, so there's no confusion on how this little kid with his delicate curls, who is not yet ten years old, will definitely grow up to be something super masculine. The McManns probably dream of a star quarterback with a name like Titan. They'd be beside themselves to picture any future other than one carved out in blue eyes and all-American ideals.

The girls were a little older than Titan, but they always let him and his friend tag along with them. In the winter, they seemed to favor the garden shed as a hangout. The shed's door creaked loudly when opened and shut, and if Daisy or I were working from home that day, one of us would peer out the window to see what the kids were up to. I'm not sure why. Morbid curiosity, perhaps, at this new residential life surrounding us. We'd both come from rural worlds and isolated homes. Watching the neighbors became a strange entertainment—and it seemed harmless when we realized the kids were sneaking in a Ouija board. Like a rite of preadolescent childhood.

"Good for them," I had said over the winter. "Seeking out the occult young."

Daisy raised an eyebrow. "I guess that's one way for them to rebel against suburbia."

Something happened in that shed. One night, the kids screamed and ran out. None of them held the board, so it must have been left behind. The group of four bolted into the McManns' house and never set foot in the shed again.

What had happened? They all seemed too freaked out for just one of them to have pranked the others.

The idea of those kids summoning something real… it was a silly thought. Until the winter evenings grew longer and strange groans emitted from the shed. Daisy and I watched, for several nights, as flashes of light broke through beneath the door. None of the McManns had entered the shed for weeks, but something stirred within those wooden walls.

I brought it up once to June and Freddy.

"Eh, McMann probably sneaks off there at night to watch porn," Freddy said. June slapped him on the arm and marched him back inside, but I thought it was a possibility.

At least, until an hour ago. They'd waited all winter, these clever gnomes, until spring broke open with a warm yoke of a sun. It dripped shining rays all over town, and like clockwork cockroaches, people scurried out their front doors. They hung up spring-themed wreaths and laid down flower-patterned welcome mats. An unspoken competition existed here, of who could have the most beautiful lawn as spring pushed onward. Who would have the brightest tulips and greenest grass? The most neatly trimmed hedges? Mulch and decorative rocks arrived in truckloads, as uniform as any army tank invasion.

"Babe," Daisy had asked me yesterday. "Should we be getting a garden together?" She gnawed on her fingernails and looked at me with worry in those pretty brown eyes.

I'd shrugged, not much of the garden type, but I told her I'd be happy to try and plant flowers or herbs with her. I didn't feel too confident in my ability not to kill every plant I touched, though.

This morning, it turns out a garden is the least of our worries. Daisy glances away from the window after calling the gnomes creepy. I'm working at my desk by the window and glimpse downward where Mrs. McMann has several gnomes lined up to carefully place in the garden bed she's plotting. She was the first McMann to step foot in the shed for weeks, and she seems to be okay.

Her gnomes are of the more tasteful variety, compared to vulgar ones I've seen in the past on shelves or online. This neighborhood doesn't seem the type to boast gnomes with their trousers down and clay asses out, or the ones flipping you off.

Mrs. McMann's are performing helpful tasks. One dressed in teal overalls gives a smile and holds a bluebird; another in a pointy green hat pulls on a tiny wheelbarrow with tinier rocks inside. An almost-cute guy, with its face covered by an orange hat and big white beard, playfully climbs over a painted mushroom. They don't seem sinister, until one holding a watering can moves away from the others, then looks directly up at us.

"No way," I say and duck. "They can't really see us?"

Daisy slowly peeks back out and makes a kind of garbled noise. "It's happened. It really happened."

We'd discussed this, as senseless as it seemed. The idea of something in the shed growing sentient over the winter.

We didn't suspect gnomes until we watched Mrs. McMann haul them out this morning.

"Those kids contacted some kind of spirit and left it to grow in the shed for weeks."

"Shit, Daisy. You really think so? I mean, I guess any kid would go running and screaming. They aren't, like, hunters of the supernatural."

"I know, it's just bonkers. Maybe we imagined that gnome moving."

We look at each other, and as we move to check the window again, Mrs. McMann lets out a gutting scream. The gnome with the wheelbarrow is chucking tiny rocks at her face. She stares and then screams for another beat before she grabs her trowel and bolts.

The other gnomes sprint around the garden bed. Daisy opens the window, and peculiar whispers drift in. I don't recognize the language, but the gnomes are chattering in a way that makes my heart race. Fear creeps up my chest as the creatures move, spreading their odd language around the neighborhood. The gnomes speak to Mrs. McMann's ceramic frogs, and they spring to life. With red eyes and distorted ribbits, they hop around the yard, as if searching for something.

Mr. McMann emerges, examining the yard for what his wife is screaming about, and the gnomes and frogs dart in unison toward him.

There's a moment where I want to lock the door, take shelter with Daisy, and let the neighborhood fend for itself, but I keep thinking about June and Freddy. Their kindness, how they welcomed us.

"We have to warn them."

Daisy nods. She doesn't need me to elaborate because she's already thinking the same thing, and my heart swells a little more with love. Mr. McMann seems to have made it back inside the house, but the gnomes and frogs are launching themselves at the sliding door in the back. The crack of glass is like a gunshot.

"Do we have any weapons?"

"I have pepper spray," Daisy says and grabs her purse, retrieving the spray.

I run downstairs and grab the two biggest kitchen knives I can find, then hand one to Daisy.

"What else would hurt supernatural gnomes?"

"Well," I say as I rummage through the cabinet below the kitchen sink. "We have wasp killer." I arm myself with Raid and woefully wonder how we'll ever survive any type of apocalypse.

I follow Daisy to the front door, which she opens with deliberate care—just a crack to hear if there's any commotion out front, but it seems isolated to the back-yard, for now. As we step onto the paved walkway, I'm hit with a stench of sour sulfur between the spring blooms.

"It smells like a funeral home," Daisy says. I nod in agreement and then halt my movements as the whispers drift through the air again.

"Do you hear that?"

Daisy's face goes pale in answer. She points to the houses down Oleander Drive. The gnomes run between front porches and garden sheds with clumsy speed. Their strange spell twists through lawns and upturned earth, possessing any lawn ornament in its path. These bastards learned more than we thought while they were cooped up in the shed.

The screeching honk of a goose echoes through the air.

"Oh no," I say, realizing where I've seen a goose before on Oleander Drive.

It comes stomping down the road from someone's front porch, hissing. Its stone feet leave cracks in the asphalt.

"Come on." Daisy nudges me, and we move toward June and Freddy's house. More screams erupt down the drive as neighbors discover their garden curios have come to life with hellish intent.

I spy two heads through the front window and knock on the door. Freddy peeks through the glass and then ushers us inside the entrance.

"Hurry up now."

He locks the door while June walks over to us, eyeing our knives and sprays.

"Oh girls, that's sad. Don't you have a real weapon?" She grabs a shotgun off their coffee table and beams at the thing. "This here is Betty."

I don't really like guns, but Betty's long-barreled grin seems like a solid defense against the gnomes and the damned goose.

June laughs at my open-mouthed facial expression. "Didn't think we were gun people, did ya?"

"Not really."

Freddy's carrying some kind of pistol as he moves around the house, securing windows and checking doors. I move aside a curtain decorated in a raspberry pattern and peer outside, spying more ceramic frogs. They're taller than Mrs. McMann's, and wearing straw hats. One carries a very sharp pitchfork while the other drives a tractor down the road. They must be a part of some farm-themed set.

The tractor driver runs over a gnome, decapitating it. Maybe they'll tear each other apart if left alone long enough, but I'm not sure if we have the time to wait.

"What's the plan?" Freddy asks June.

"Well, we could hunker down. Let the neighbors fend for themselves. Lord knows they wouldn't come to our defense, but I hate the thought of some satanic garden critters taking over the neighborhood. This used to be a nice place."

Daisy shrugs. "It *is* nice. You both are nice. Even people like the McManns shouldn't be taken out by a freaky gnome."

"Alright girls," Freddy says, everything serious in that sun-kissed, wrinkled face. They'd been in Florida two weeks ago, and I suddenly remember the plastic flamingo decorations they brought back and set outside. Did they come to life, too?

"June and I will lead. Let's go see if we can find the McManns and their kids. If something comes at you, use those sprays first and then stab."

"Spray and stab," I repeat. "Got it."

"Let's move."

The flamingos find us first.

"Watch out!" Daisy yells. She dodges out of the way, but one flamingo's beak grazes her shoulder, drawing blood.

June jumps between them and blasts the flamingos right in their little plastic bodies. It doesn't take much to waste them into bubblegum-bright confetti, but the noise attracts a whole horde of gnomes.

Why these two elderly hippies are so ready for war, I have no idea. I think June's from Tennessee, but I'm not sure of Freddy's background. Either way, I don't question it. I'm just glad we're on the same side.

"You okay?" I reach for Daisy.

She nods. "It stings but isn't a deep cut."

We all duck behind the back deck, and spot Mrs. McMann. She's securing the garden shed with some kind of aluminum lockout, and I take a guess that she's ushered her children inside. How cruel the place that originated this madness is now the safe house for the kids. I can't help but wonder what they summoned, and how, but it doesn't matter now.

She's limping, face scratched up, and I want to call out to her, but the gnomes get there first. They've commandeered some of the bigger clay frogs into being their rides. Like cowboys with long white beards bucking up and down on amphibian broncos.

June and Freddy take aim.

"Dammit," Freddy says. "Can't get a good shot. They're too close to her."

"Don't shoot that woman," June says. "We don't need to go to *jail* for her."

"You have bad blood with the McManns?" I ask, too curious to stop myself despite the way Daisy frowns at me.

June snorts. "She's a menace. Tried to have us evicted several times for our color choices on the house and fence. Claimed we were doing drugs. Maybe we should let her fend for herself."

Still, they steady their weapons. I know they don't want the possessed creatures to win, despite their dealings with Mrs. McMann.

But there isn't much we can do. They've swarmed.

"Spray and stab!" Daisy yells, and she sprints through the grass, pepper spray at the ready. I grumble and follow her, shaking my can of Raid.

"Oh, for fuck's sake," Freddy shouts behind us, but he and June scramble across the grass, too.

The gnomes, with their bright hats and flower-embroidered shirts, swarm like a rainbow of wasps until Mrs. McMann stops crawling across the yard. I aim the Raid away from her face and try to go after the ones on her torso and legs. Daisy kicks a chipped frog out of the way and starts stomping on whatever she can. The gnomes claw at her pants, climbing up Daisy's body.

"Watch out!" June yells, and I dive out of the way, afraid of the shotgun, but instead she's turned on the McManns' hose to full blast. A powerful spray *wooshes* from the hose and knocks a few creeps off Daisy.

Have you ever heard a garden gnome scream? It's pretty fucking weird. Like angry baby rabbits possessed by weed-whackers. Tiny weapons get blasted from their hands, and many of them scatter, taking their minions and frogs with them. Others fall down, remain dazed on the lawn.

"You good?"

Daisy nods, so I bend to check on Mrs. McMann, who is definitely not good. My heart sinks as I realize it's too late to help her. The gnomes have stuffed her mouth with small, colorful rocks, all the way down her throat. Her eyes, too, brim with the pebbles. Wet, pointy hats from the gnomes stick to her clothes like decorative Velcro.

"She isn't breathing." Daisy tries to dig the rocks out of Mrs. McMann's mouth, but they're never-ending. Infinitely filled. The spring sun, uncaring of the carnage, glints down and shines on something in Mrs. McMann's loose grip.

I take the key from her cooling fingers.

"Honey?" a weak voice asks, and I turn to see Mr. McMann lurching from the house. The glass door is nothing more than a shattered memory. His shoes crunch over the glass, and blood trickles down from his temple. He must have been knocked out. When he sees his wife, the man's knees buckle, and he falls into a sobbing heap on the grass.

"I'm sorry, Mr. McMann."

I don't see it until it's already on his shoulder, the garden gnome with the small trowel. It wastes no time in sticking the weapon right into Mr. McMann's throat.

Daisy pepper sprays the small beast. It screams and runs off with frightening speed, but Freddy destroys the thing with a perfect shot. Bits of clay shatter and rain down onto the grass, but none of that will help Mr. McMann.

"Promise us," he says, clutching his throat as it gushes. "You'll keep the children safe. They're yours now." His voice is then lost in a gargle of blood.

Daisy, more soft-hearted than I, tells Mr. McMann we'll find their aunt or uncle or someone.

Mr. McMann shakes his head. "Yours now."

"What? We don't want your kids."

"Brooke!" Daisy gives me a look, and I hush, but I give her a look back that says, *fine, lie to the dying man.*

And he does die, watching us argue while blood jets out onto the lawn.

I turn to Daisy. "We aren't really taking three kids, are we?"

"God, no," she says and shudders. "We'll find the next of kin, though. We can do that."

"Sure. If we get out of here alive."

Screeching fills the air, and I turn to see an army. Angry gnomes carrying little gardening tools; hopping frogs that were once peaceful garden bed displays; the titanic chunk of stone goose; rabbits wearing strawberry sweaters, mouths foaming…

"Run!" Freddy commands while June fires. There's nothing like a shotgun blast to get your ass moving.

A large paper butterfly is beating itself against the window of the garden shed, attracting the attention of the gnomes. They know the kids are in there.

I grab Daisy and direct her to the shed. My shaking hands can barely get the key into the lock, but Daisy places her fingers on mine and together, we open the door.

Three petrified children look out at us from within the shed, their wide eyes enough to melt your heart, if you had the time. We don't.

"Come on!" I bark. They'll die if they stay in there, and they might die out here, but at least out in the open they aren't caged animals, waiting for an inevitable end.

"Help us!" McKarty screams.

"Shush! Keep your voices down," I say. June and Freddy emerge behind us, guns pointed at the yard. "What's going on out there?"

"A few neighbors have joined the fight, but we gotta keep moving," Freddy says.

"Hey," Daisy uses a gentle voice with the kids. "Your parents wanted us to take care of you, but we're going to try to find your aunts or uncles, okay?"

The girls nod. The boy, Titan, cries.

"Any of you know how to shoot?" June asks.

They shake their heads.

"Dammit." Freddy digs in his bag. "I have some pocket-knives. Do the best you can."

"We want to go home," Kayleigha says between sobs, and snot drips down from her nose onto her pastel pink dress. The girls look to be about twelve, but they're so helpless. These perfectly posh creatures, with their shiny hair and clean fingernails. How the hell did they summon anything so dark and cruel, this thing that has taken over the gnomes and created a horrible haunting of lawn ornaments to destroy the neighborhood?

"Well, your folks are dead, and you summoned whatever the hell this is, so too bad. You're fighting," I say. It's a bit harsh, but frankly, I'm exhausted.

"We didn't mean to," they all say in unison, and it freaks me out.

Freddy arms them with pocketknives, and we sneak around the McManns' house to join a few others down Oleander Drive. There are bodies on the road, both human and garden decorations. The mighty stone goose is beak-deep in some poor person's gutted stomach. Blood and goop cover its face as the goose rises, marches toward us with its ceramic and clay army, all these once innocent ornaments still possessed by something angry and hungry.

I look to Daisy, and she grabs her knife and pepper spray tight. The goose marches forward.

"Spray and stab," I say, shaking my Raid.

She smiles, kisses me for luck. "Spray and stab."

THE REVENGE OF RAPPACCINI'S DAUGHTER

"I am going, father, where the evil which thou hast striven to mingle with my being will pass away like a dream—like the fragrance of these poisonous flowers, which will no longer taint my breath among the flowers of Eden. Farewell, Giovanni! Thy words of hatred are like lead within my heart; but they, too, will fall away as I ascend. Oh, was there not, from the first, more poison in thy nature than in mine?"

—"Rappaccini's Daughter"
Nathaniel Hawthorne

I. Creation

I do not blame my father for burying me.

Even as I struggle to escape this dirt womb, mud caked beneath my nails, I don't find blame in my heart. Does a heart still exist within a resurrected body?

Withered lungs or not, my breath grows heavy between the loam. I never did care for confined spaces; funny, given how I barely left the garden or our home when I was alive, not that my father gave me many choices.

I am not buried very deep, and perhaps this is my salvation. If I truly needed air, I would have suffocated long ago during this uncomfortable unconsciousness in smothering darkness.

Finally, my fingers stretch up, beyond ground, and I claw out from my tomb. Bright sunlight overpowers my vision and turns the world into a color-streaked blur. I crawl forward, palms landing on cool, flat stones, and I know I am near the fountain ruins. Dry blinks and a weighty heaving freeze me in place for several moments. My vision returns in jagged slowness, like soggy puzzle pieces drying out.

I drag myself to the one remaining stone bench on the fountain, which sits in the center of the botanic garden. Despite the chaos of the broken stones, water gushes from the center, babbling happily beneath beams of sun. Relief settles somewhere inside me when I inhale the familiar scent of fragrant blooms and earthy shrubs. Aromas that danced with me since childhood, and now, even in my death. My after-death. Whatever this is… Perhaps some cruel purgatory come to show me how I will never escape my father's garden.

The harsh sun dulls behind a cloud, and I take in the scenery of a madman's jungle. At least, that's how it always appeared to outsiders. To me, it's still *home*.

Blossoms of purple sprout between giant leaves, and there, a familiar wreath of Queen Anne's lace around the statue of Vertumnus. Gods of the garden, have you summoned me back? By all scientific accounts, I was dead, and Signor Dr. Giacomo Rappaccini is a great man of science and medicine; so, who would have argued with him that his only daughter had fallen lifeless at his very feet? His only child. His most precious experiment. Gone.

And gone I should have remained. Instead, it seems destiny planted my bulb of a corpse only for me to rebloom. Roots and all, I have emerged from the soil bed. So, I tell myself again, I do not blame my father for burying me, but I do blame him for the path that led to my young demise. While he fancied himself a creator, in several different ways, he was also a fool. It seemed ill providence would send several foolish men to me, and I, poor Beatrice, did not yet know how to navigate the world of men.

An unpleasant tickle in my throat forces me to gag, and out come dirt and dead worms. I pull maggots from my ears and hair. None of them wriggle. At this sight, there is little surprise. When I lived, bright beetles would find me, as did lizards, spiders, and a number of other victims. Attracted to the perfumes of the hybrid flowers my father created, strange twists of hydrangeas and mountain laurels, foxglove spires mated with devil's helmet, and on and on it went. Then of course, they became attracted to me. For was I not also a hybrid in this wicked place?

If the creatures crawled across my neck or hands, any exposed part of skin, or even breathed in the same air I exhaled, they would curl up to perish. Poor souls. How many times did I cross myself here, praying for the lives of butterflies and frogs?

I glance down at my flesh now, only a little is exposed where insects tried to eat away at my gloves and the long sleeves of my gown. Removing my gloves, I find normal skin, a bit paler than when I lived, but I expected to discover much worse. How long have I been beneath the ground? I am not decomposed, nor bruised with blue. No bones uncovered. Only my gown shows tatters, and I suppose that's how far the insects of the grave managed to get. I cannot blame the flies and their friends for trying to find nourishment within my body, but instead it seems they only found more grief. Even dead, I seep toxins.

If this is what my father, my creator, wanted…then soon he shall also know this taste.

My entire world has been confined to my father's garden, his exquisite Eden of poisonous flowers. What else is there to tell of my story? Very little, I suppose, other than my loneliness and profound sadness, and those have always tasted more bitter to me than poison.

Some have heard of me, mostly through the tales of my father. He is quite the famous botanist, even in his old age, and his strange penchant for distilling plants into medicines, of a sort, was not a thing done in secret. He was proud of his experiments. I don't think many knew I was such an intimate part of the work; I was just a pretty daughter, locked away in Rappaccini's garden, unknown and unable to be known by the outside world.

What am I, truly? I know not. I never had a choice in my becoming. I was birthed by a mother who departed this earthly realm shortly after my first breaths. Upon seeing my mother grow weak and die, my father vowed that his daughter would become something strong. Something fearsome, even.

Then by default, something wretched.

I inherited my mother's great beauty, and I fear, my father's great madness. I recall his words, before my death, before he knew about the vial. My almost-lover, Giovanni, presented the vial to me, as he believed the drink would reverse my father's work. As if anything could be so enchanted as to rid one's blood and flesh and heart from poison.

Before that, I had exclaimed my loneliness and misery. Shouted it to Vertumnus and to the deadly nightshade, to the ivy on the walls and to the wide sky.

"Misery," he had replied, "to be as terrible as thou art beautiful?"

Misery, I think, *has come to greet me once again.* The vial from Giovanni did not cure me. It did not reverse my dangerous touch, did not allow me to ever kiss him.

Weariness lives in my bones, regardless of whatever I am now, but then I see her. Oh, how delight finds me once again. My one fleeting connection to happiness.

"Sister!"

I run to her, my bosom a starburst of joy as we embrace. Though it seems I have no heart to beat within my rib-cage, any remaining trace of humanity within my being beats for her.

Sister.

The precious purple gems hanging from her jade leaves are more beautiful than ever. Such a royal hue, even Giovanni had trouble resisting the want to touch her flowers. Still, I hold this plant with all the affection of humans who love one another. Her breath perfumes into me, and I am grateful to inhale her sweet scent. It is the aroma of my childhood and my whole livelihood. Our shared breath. My father always told me she sprang to life upon my birth, and together we grew and flourished.

She is the secret to my existence. From infancy, I have been envenomed by her. This entire kingdom of horticultural insanity raised me, fed me, thrived within me. I, too, am toxic and rare.

"Oh, sister," I say and sigh, content to stand here with her, but the joyful reunion is cut short when I see it. A morbid reminder of my death. Clouds part, and a gleam of sunshine surrounds the silver vial.

It looks like such an innocent thing, far more innocent than anything else in this garden. The same silver vial I drank from, brought to me by the one who longed for me most. When I think of Giovanni now, his name sticks on my tongue like rotten pomegranate seeds. Did he even miss me? Had he moved on? I had no idea how long I'd stayed beneath the soil.

The vial rests on the wooden shelves where Father keeps his gardening tools and thick gloves. Only I can touch the most dangerous plants with bare hands. Dust and cobwebs have overtaken the shears and watering pots, which is unusual. I can't help but think something terrible has happened to my father if he hasn't been out here taking care of the plants with his customary diligence.

I hate how my hand trembles when I reach for the silver vial, but I have to touch it. Do I tremble from fear or anger? Perhaps a mixture boils my blood, but I doubt I even have blood anymore. I think I'm made only of toxins and strange flesh that feels more like the leaves of a hydrangea than skin.

Still, I open the vial and peer inside. I know by its lightness that it must be empty or nearly so, and I hear no slosh of remaining liquid. Could Giovanni have swallowed down the rest of the potion, or did my father do something with it?

I want to know—I want to see the look on all of their faces when they behold the return of Beatrice Rappaccini. The taste of resentment is bitter on my tongue, but I hold it between my teeth as I creep up the stone stairs that lead like a sculptured portal into the house.

Giovanni once told me how he would watch, from the gloomy window of his room, how I appeared and disappeared beneath the stone arch covered in vines and orange flowers. He made it sound much more magical. In reality, I stumble up these stairs, still a little weak, into the unlocked house. Swirls of dust follow my hem, and I trace grime along the banisters and walls. Dirt trails my footsteps as I make my way to my father's study. Has he fired the lone housekeeper we kept? Did she break her promises to withhold our secrets from the public?

He is not at his desk, which might be for the best, because I have not yet decided what I shall do upon seeing him.

I am familiar with the thick leather journal on my father's desk. It's stamped in faded gold lettering that reads *The Journal of Dr. Giacomo Rappaccini*—a text as sacred to him as any religious tome. He'd spend hours writing in it, but only let me read certain sections with supervision. For hours, I'd absorb myself fully into learning every plant's scientific name, what medicinal purpose it could possess, or often, what deadly poison it harbored. Those pages I was allowed to lose myself in, but never the pages about me.

About my poisons.

"Ask me anything, Beatrice, and I shall tell you," my father would say when I asked to read more on my origin and how my sister and I kept each other alive. He told me the basics, how I was offspring of his flesh, and how she was offspring of his botanical intellect. Together, we sustained one another.

He was an expert in avoiding the details I craved. I doubt the journal would hold any answers to who I am now, but still, curiosity lures me closer, and I settle in Father's creaking chair. Cradling the book with all the tenderness of a newborn sprout, I turn over pages and pages.

Sticky disappointment settles low my belly. Many of the pages have been torn out. The ones about me.

All the details of the plants remain, of the medicines and amalgams in the garden. Calculations and science that he taught me only through a filtered lens. I try to decipher them now in the journal, but anger clouds over any rationality I have left. Toward the journal's end, though, a few pages show bright ink and hurried handwriting…

He wrote of my death. From the entry dates, I gather I have been buried for about a month:

> *The accursed liquid potion from an accursed man. Baglioni has long since been jealous of my work, and his greatest punishment is my greatest pain. Beatrice is no more, having taken the vial from her foolish Giovanni, who should have loved and protected her. I made a study of the man, and I convinced myself Giovanni would change to become like Beatrice. He almost had. I needed more time to complete him, this companion for my daughter. He was not ready to give up the normal life of mankind for her, but he was nearly there.*

> *Instead, Baglioni brought ruin down upon us all. If he had discussed this plan with me, I could have told him the "antidote" he offered would not render virulent poisons into something harmless, not for Beatrice. Nothing on this earth can reverse what Beatrice is, nourished with the plants from her birth and upward. She is the very essence of transformation. Morphed by more than my hands and the plants—she is lightning and stardust. Bound to the secrets of the universe in ways even I cannot discover.*

> *That vial was the true poison, causing her to suffer into an early grave.*

> *Perhaps the antidote will work on Giovanni, but from my studies it seems extremely weak. A cure created by a man who only thinks he knows what he is doing.*

*But I confess, whatever Giovanni's life becomes now,
I do not care. My intellectual curiosity is too buried
beneath a deep depression of Beatrice's absence.*

Rancor churns within me as I set the journal down. I never asked where Giovanni got the vial from, that cursed antidote. I was so eager to become what he wanted me to be, a normal girl for him to love. I drank the potion down, and the world swirled before me in gray gloom, stealing all the prismatic colors of the garden away.

Baglioni. I know this name. Professor Pietro Baglioni, another man of medicine. His repute is known widely, like my father's, but he was always more straightforward. An old, jovial man who could talk of great philosophies and ideas, but did not have the mind to create the way my father did.

Though, apparently, he had attempted to create something to save Giovanni. Was he so precious to the professor, whereas I meant so little? He had clearly aimed to take Giovanni away, the only one who has ever dared enter the garden to speak to me. If Giovanni had drank the antidote first, it might have saved him, and he would have left. Such an event would have wrought my heart into tortured despair, but I know I would have survived it.

My death at the hands of this man, of all these men, corrodes my toxic resins into a blush of anger. I never allowed myself to experience much anger before; it seemed unnecessary given the direction of my abnormal, secluded life. Now that I have a taste for it, the adrenaline does not seem willing to let me go.

A shattering of glass echoes around the study, and I swirl to face the entry where my father stands, a broken dish at his feet. He gapes openly in pale astonishment, standing in his usual scholarly garb of black.

"As I live and breathe, dear Beatrice, precious daughter. Is that you? Are you a ghost come to haunt me, come to escort me to the underworld I so surely belong in? My Beatrice must have ascended into heavenly realms, for she was innocent. Innocent!"

"I have ascended into nothing, Father. Poor Beatrice, buried but not dead. Poor Beatrice, forced to become something poisonous without love. Poor Beatrice." My voice is venom when I spit out my own name, and I have never spoken to my father like this. Nor have I felt more connected to the fatal science in my veins and breath. My very soul soured by it.

Born from poison and grief, molded by a father who fancied himself the type of creator who could harvest lightning from storm clouds.

He shuffles closer, as if approaching a wounded animal. "Daughter, what is happening in your head?"

"Tell me, am I girl or monster?"

"You are Beatrice," he says and then shakes his head. "My Beatrice."

A cold laugh slithers from my throat. "Who wants to hear of Beatrice the girl when they can instead hear of Beatrice the monster?"

He doesn't know what to say, and I find a strange satisfaction in that. Rarely was my father ever speechless in all of these years.

"Where does this Professor Baglioni live?"

"That is what you ask?" He stands before me, face wrinkled as an ancient tree, eyes still searching in disbelief. "Are you a spirit?"

I hold out my hand across the desk. "Touch me and find out."

He cannot. No one can hold my hand without painful blisters rising onto their flesh. Or worse.

"It was that foolish youth who took you from me. He should have thrown the vial antidote back at Baglioni and been done with it."

"Do not blame Giovanni entirely, sir. For was it not you who set us all on this path? You used Giovanni as an experiment, as you did to me. You entranced him and knew we would fall in love and never be able to let anything come of it."

"You misremember!" He grumbles and shakes his walking stick. "Giovanni was becoming a gift for you, something entirely yours. Together you could have loved for years, perhaps forever. But that idiot boy, too afraid to love. Too afraid to change into something greater. He was the one who refused you, the real you."

"The real me?" I slam the journal shut and stand to face him. "Tell me again, is that monster or daughter?"

"I have never imagined you as a monster. Never! You may inspire horror in others, Beatrice, but that is their problem. It was never meant to be yours. I knew someday a lad would come along and love you completely, and I am sorry that I thought Giovanni was that person. If I knew of his cowardice, how it would consume him, I would not have allowed him to continue his visits in the garden and become your true companion."

Frustration dries my tongue. "Companionship should not be the result of an experiment, Father. Love should not be created from the science of vials and poison. Enough of this. You continue to speak of Giovanni so that you do not have to face your own actions."

He stares at me, words bubbling up behind his teeth, but he still has not seemed to decide if I am real or a dream. Then, a question floats like pollen into my head, and I reluctantly bring the conversation back to Giovanni.

"Did he drink the antidote, too? I read your entry here."

Father shrugs. "Not after seeing you fall. He went a bit mad, and I took the antidote away to study it, but I am sure Baglioni had more to give the boy. I did not care enough to inquire after either of them. I descended into such low darkness after you died. Loneliness, my only friend. The housekeeper resigned and bolted away in the night. I think my ramblings finally frightened her away."

"Giovanni is gone from the apartment?" I look out the window, only able to see a corner of the old mansion across from the garden where Giovanni had once stayed. Where he had gazed at me from the window, waved and called to me. Tossed fresh bouquets down, only for them to wither in the clutch.

"He moved elsewhere. Beatrice, listen to me—"

"I have done enough listening, Father." I turn and move past him. "We are not finished here."

I leave while words still dangle from his lips. The longer I stay, the more tempting it becomes to place a palm against his cheek and let my poisons burn him. It is something I cannot do. There is still a love of sorts I hold for the old man, a kinship cradled within my rotten ribcage; he did tend to me with affection over the years, but I will never know if it was for the love of his daughter or his experiment. How cruel a thing, to become your only surviving parent's bit of research, never certain if your death only brought sadness because it ended the experiment early.

While living, I never let myself ruminate too long on those thoughts, fearing they would send my mind into a darkness I could not escape. I chose the sunrise instead, the view of glistening dewdrops on the plants in the morning. I chose to absorb any happiness I could, but now, post-death, those shadowed thoughts turn darker, and have come to haunt me.

II. Judgment

I swap my tattered death gown for another dress, an old favorite dyed with an ombre of purple. A fair contrast to my black funeral dress, though I am sure I had no funeral. No mourners, outside of my father and perhaps Giovanni. I pick up an oversized hat with a veil attached around the brim. Before I died, I could talk to my father and Giovanni without my very breath hurting them, but I always kept a distance. The danger was always in kissing me, getting too close. Since I died, however, that power feels stronger, and I fear killing an innocent person who has never once talked to me.

With an addition of long gloves and clean shoes, I exit the house. In the past, I have not really been beyond the garden. When I was very young, Father took me to a few parks and spots out in nature, but never into town. I think of myself as educated, but only by books and music, paintings and history. Father claimed people would gawk, try to touch me. If my poisons hurt them, or even killed them, I would be taken away.

Now as I walk alone, I blend in well enough. I keep a distance, careful not to bump into anyone. There are some glances from both ladies and men, but I can't tell what they're thinking. Do they know I've died, or am I just oddly dressed on this warm day? I find myself staring at a young couple, walking arm in arm. Her in a buttery dress and matching parasol, and the man in finely tailored trousers and coat. They are a striking pair, and I admit to the jealousy radiating within me, but there is also hope. A tiny root of it, always growing somewhere in my mind, and perhaps this is my biggest folly.

I walk along cobbled streets and gander at the colorful storefronts, the stone walls, the everyday people, a beautiful woman selling flowers I cannot touch without withering their blooms. Fresh-baked bread and pastries send mouthwatering scents into the streets. I long to grin and speak with others, but I keep my rubied lips sealed tight. To breathe in my perfumed air is too dangerous for the common person.

I do not have far to go to visit the home of Professor Pietro Baglioni. I came across his last known address in an old contact book I swiped from my father's office. Before I knock, I pull down the veil from my hat, hoping it keeps the housekeeper safe enough from breathing in my poisons. I explain myself as a student of medicine, and though she gives me an uneasy glance, she lets me inside.

"Signor Baglioni is so wise," she says. "I'm sure he will help you with your questions."

"Thank you," I say, but I have studied medicinal properties of my father's plants, and I know more about poisons than this professor ever shall. These things I long to say, but politeness, as it ever did, holds me as its prisoner.

I am led to a small study, dimly lit and stacked with books, antiques, globes, and many fine things.

"A visitor," I hear the housekeeper say. "A student."

The door creaks open, and in steps an older man with a smile on his face. Dark curls sit atop his head, paired with bushy brows. He appears to be a little younger than my father and in far better spirits. Father spoke occasionally about this colleague, but it was not a subject that brought him joy. Their disagreements were of harsh natures, from what I understand.

"Who is there?" he asks, the smile wavering for a moment as I look up from the shadows.

"Just a girl," I say. "A girl you killed."

He is so pale and still that I think perhaps my very visage has frightened him to death. Finally, he blinks.

This man of science and rationale, how does he justify the resurrection of Beatrice Rappaccini?

"Are you a phantom?"

I stand up and browse the shelves of books. Dull titles with faded covers. "I'm not sure what I am. I used to think I knew, but then you poisoned me with a drug meant to reverse poisons. Funny."

He stumbles over to the desk, grabs onto the edges for stability. "You were buried."

"You know, for too long, I told myself I could never be as bright as my father. How could I ever understand what exactly he creates? He is something of a genius, as I'm sure you have heard."

"Rappaccini is a madman. Are you not proof of that?"

I spin around, brow furrowed. "You're quite daring to anger a *phantom*."

He shakes his head. "I tried to help you. The concoction was only meant to reverse what your father contaminated Giovanni with, and hopefully you as well. You say I killed you, but here you stand."

Fear wafts from this man with a stale-sweat odor. I can taste it in the air. Good. He should be afraid. I walk closer and remove my gloves. His eyes widen as if he expects to see some bubbling purple flesh, but by all accounts, my hands appear normal. He's still sizing me up, trying to piece together if I really died and came back, or never died at all.

"Where is Giovanni? Does he live?"

Baglioni nods. "He is getting better, no thanks to your father."

"What do you mean?"

"Rappaccini took the antidote I distilled from such precious herbs. And with it, the rest of the liquid that was meant to cure Giovanni from your poisoning. I had to make a new batch, and it took longer than I had hoped. Now he is recovering, but not yet cured."

I wish I had more time to absorb this news, to let it sink in how quickly Giovanni wanted to go back to being a normal man. Someone who was willing to change me to suit his worldview, but who refused to change at all for me. Would a compromise have ever been possible?

No. The answer echoes in my head. *Not in this scenario.*

"You had no idea what the potion would do to me, yet still you encouraged Giovanni to bewitch me with it, to promise me a life together if I drank it down. I remember the burning taste, how it seared through my chest. I withered inside, the entire time I remained underground. Buried but not dead. Waiting to crawl back up from the earth when I was strong enough. The gods of the garden have returned me to this earth, and I have not come back with a forgiving heart."

"What madness pours from your tongue? You are your father's daughter, after all."

He looks back to the study door, not completely closed. A caged old bear looking for an exit.

"Perhaps I am mad," I say. "Or perhaps I understand the ways of men with astounding clarity, and that is what you fear the most."

Baglioni shakes his head, clenches and unclenches his hands from nerves. "Foolish child."

I don't wish to draw this out, so I walk to the professor without my veil. The perfume of my flesh lingers in the air, bringing with it an almost sleepy haze. He breathes in deeply, and then realizes he shouldn't have. I am still learning all of my capabilities, but for the first time, I feel powerful. Baglioni itches to flee from me, but instead he falls into the hypnotic scent of my rose-rich breath, and I reach out a hand to cradle his face. Another hand around his throat.

He gasps, feeling my toxins already dancing into his bloodstream. How quickly I can pollute. The warmth of his cheek against my palm blisters. The enamel of his molars melts to his cheek, and I pull away. His windpipe fills with noxious liquids, and he lets forth a garbling song.

I could have kept my fingertips pressed to his neck. This quick death, it is hardly a suffering.

"This is a blessing," I say, and as he gapes at me wide-eyed, gurgling, I turn to leave. It is not unlike what he did to me, planting the vial in Giovanni's hands alongside impossible promises.

I promise nothing, but I linger in the doorway before I close it.

"Goodbye, professor. May death be kinder to you than it was to me."

Outside the study, I nearly walk into the housekeeper carrying a tray with two cups of tea. With hurried hands, I pull my veil back over my face.

"Oh, I'm so sorry! The professor just dozed off. I tried to leave quietly."

The woman smiles at me, and her warmth is lovely as sun. "He dozes often these days. Working too hard, I say. Well, if you'd like a cup of tea, please feel free to linger and enjoy."

"Thank you, but I best be going. I need to find an old friend, and I'm afraid I have no idea where he is staying."

"Signora, what is this friend's name? We receive many visitors here, so perhaps I can help."

"He is a handsome man, with good cheekbones and a welcoming manner. Giovanni Guasconti."

Her eyes light up, so eager to help. "Why miss, Signor Guasconti is upstairs recovering from an illness. Professor Baglioni has been most diligent attending to him."

My heart no longer contains the ability to flutter, but something whispers throughout my system. Something exciting. I do not overlook this serendipitous gift and know the garden gods must have brought me back. Must have led me here to complete another step in the trinity that will unlock freedom.

The attentive housekeeper, bless her, leads me up to Giovanni's room. She knocks first and opens the door a sliver.

"Signor, you have a visitor."

III. The Lovers

I'm not sure what to feel when I first see him. His back is toward me as he gazes out the window at the bustling life of northern Italy. A thick blanket pools around his shoulders despite the summer weather. In the month of my absence, he seems to have aged ten years, but his softness remains, his handsomeness. The waves of golden hair that so contrast with my black tresses.

When he turns to face me, we are both startled. Him, obviously because I am supposed to be dead. As for me, I think his dark eyelids and glassy gaze will haunt me to my next grave, if I have one. I know those eyes, for they are so like mine, painted in shadows from poisonous plants having worked their way into the blood. Eyes that can lure and intoxicate, even when we don't mean them to.

"Ghost! Monster!"

The housekeeper shushes him and adjusts the blanket. I notice she does not touch his skin. Did Baglioni have the decency to warn her he might be contagious in some way? "Signor, please, this young lady wishes to speak to you. She is no monster or ghost."

Giovanni appears to take in the look of pity the woman gives him. He quiets down, resigned to some fate, I suppose. His gaze does not leave her until she exits and closes the door behind her.

"Are you afraid to be alone with me? Once upon a time, all you craved was to sit beside me on the stone bench in the garden. So close. Almost touching."

He does not stop shaking, and a great sadness flowers within my bones. I never wanted to create fear, and I never did until three men drove me into the dirt. I should not hold mercy for him, but I do. I do.

"This is how you greet me, Giovanni? After all the walks we took, the honest conversations we exchanged? You gazed at me with stars and love in your eyes, once."

Those stars have long faded and now turn to black clouds as he glares at me. "I saw you die, creature of pestilent breath and venomous skin."

"You think me a snake? I only wanted your companionship."

A hacking cough takes his breath for a moment. "You set your father out to poison me! To make me like you."

The mercy I have for him fades at these hurtful words. "I may have died, but I have not forgotten our last conversation. I told you then the truth of my sister, of my very existence. How my father nourished my sister-plant and I together. My only dream was to love you. I never set my father out to bestow his science on you and fill you with powers similar to mine. Never."

He blinks at me, and still, I cannot understand if he believes me or not. My father, on his own accord, wanted to join us in a symphony of poison and fear, but never have I been lonelier.

"You are a wretched girl, with an even more wretched father."

"So, if I offered you strength, you would not take it?"

Cold laughter plumes from his lips. "What strength could you possibly offer? I am only alive because of Baglioni."

"And I am only dead because of him. And you."

Silence. He has no smart answer to this, and a part of me hopes he feels the heat of shame in his trembling body.

"Do you not remember those walks in the garden? You almost plucked a blossom from my sister-plant, and I stopped you. Not thinking, I wrapped my fingers around your wrist to stop you. If you'd touched it, you would have died. Instead, you walked away with the burning impressions of my fingertips, like dark bruises on your skin."

A sigh so heavy, it weighs the atmosphere down. "I remember," he says. "I also remember how you haunted me in life, in dreams. The dread and horror of you matched only by your beauty, how you seduced me into your world of florae. Enticed me to want to kiss your poison lips, to taste that perfumed breath." He trails off, nostalgia and anger swirling in the particles around us.

"It is not too late to become something strong. Something like me. I am stronger than ever, and I understand myself more. I could finish what my father started, but create in better ways. Honest ways. I would never hide my intentions from you."

I hate myself for this, a last desperate plea to have someone to love by my side, but I have to try. I have to give him the choice I never had.

His eyes brighten, and he looks at me with more awareness than ever before. "I will not journey into your hell again, horrid creature. You tempt with flowers, but you hold only pestilence on your tongue and unholiness where your heart should be. Go back to your garden, where plants watch with eyes. They have always watched, always."

He's mad, I think. Or perhaps, that is what I want to believe. Easier to blame someone's cruelty on madness. The alternative slams thorns deep into my being. I am broken inside, to see what has become of this once curious and kind man who wanted nothing more than to hold my hand in an enchanted and strange garden.

"Why did you not just drink the antidote yourself and run away? You could have left me heartbroken but alive."

He does not answer my question, but I cannot stop my lips from decanting more words. This is all as I feared. My dying words come back to haunt me.

"It is true then. From the first, there has been more poison in your nature than in mine."

He looks at me as if he could spit on me, if he had the strength. These fools, they still only see me as a helpless girl. They call me "creature" and "monster" and other things, but they can't seem to fathom that I have it within me to hurt them.

"Get out of here. Leave me alone." His voice is a whisper as he turns back to the window.

"Giovanni, do you not hold yourself accountable at all for giving me that vial from the professor? They very vial that killed poor Beatrice?"

He snorts. "Poor Beatrice, indeed. No, I thought it would cure you. I have no regret about that. I only regret having ever been lured into your virulent web. I should have known, there is no saving a creature from her own poison."

"I never asked to be saved, nor created. I do not blame you entirely. I willingly drank from the toxic potion but only in hopes it would make me into someone you wanted to be with. Giovanni and Beatrice, we would have made such a lovely pair."

He says nothing else, and though I long to delay this ending, I know it's time. Still, I hesitate.

"You saw me from the window, do you remember? You told me you were so moved, so curious. You came to me. I never asked you to walk into the garden. One look, and one lustful thought, yet I am the creature of poison."

A startled squawk as I move swiftly to him and bend down, our eyes meeting. My lips on his, swallowing his breath that tickles slightly of poison, but nothing like mine. His antidote melts powerless between our shared saliva.

Hands on my waist, he grips me tight, pulls me closer for just a second before he tries to fight, but it's too late.

He gasps for the air he will never inhale again. "You taste…of Persian roses."

With that, crackles of purple web out beneath his skin as the toxins take hold, dragging him down into a depth he will never return from. Wide eyes forever open, gazing out the window.

"Goodbye, Giovanni," I whisper. Heartbreak and freedom, how they taste too similar. Too intimate. It is a strange elixir all its own. Then again, I have only ever known strangeness.

IV. Creator

My last task is the most dreaded. I knew sealing Giovanni's fate would hurt, but I feared Baglioni's weak antidote would only be temporary and draw out Giovanni's death. Once someone starts to become what I am, there is little possibility of a reversal. Only someone as mad as my father could create a true antidote.

Even though my father loves his fatal science more than I think he could ever love me, he is still the one who tended to me. Nourished me alongside my beautiful sister-plant. In the end, she will be all I have left.

Still, as I wander back through the garden, my hands invisibly stained with the lives I've taken, I fear this final task. Vertumnus awaits me, poppies growing around his head like a crown, and I swear he smiles for a moment.

"Garden gods," I say, "help me."

My sister, with all her spectacular purple gems, dances in the rippling of sunlight as evening descends. Blue mouths of wolfsbane, hellebore bred to be the deepest shade of black, Himalayan balsam swallowing a bee, and on and on the garden goes. My enigmatic sanctuary.

Father waits for me on the stone bench of the fountain ruins. This very spot, where I walked beneath the arch connecting home and garden as I greeted Giovanni. This spot so close to my grave.

I sit and join him, my gloved fingers twitching.

"You do not need those," he says, and nods toward the gloves. "Nor this." A gentle hand removes my hat.

Sadness etches an insincere smile across my face. "For your safety, I shall keep them on."

He clears his throat, reaches for my hand, and removes a glove. Our fingers intertwine, and he sighs.

"Father!" My horror does not disguise itself. Such dread makes me wonder, could I have really been the one to take his last breath? I hardly gave a second thought to sealing the fates of Baglioni, and even Giovanni once he spit his final truths. Perhaps, in some twisted way, I blamed them the most for my death rather than blaming my father.

I look into his eyes, unsure of what to say. He refuses to let me pull my venomous fingertips away from his calloused grip.

"Dearest daughter, I am already dying."

"No. Please."

I break at hearing these gentle words. Tears fall from my eyes, across my lips—the taste like poisoned honey.

"I am beyond old and weary," he continues. "I have known my days were coming to an end, and now upon seeing you again, I can close my eyes in a small contentment. You might not feel the same as you did before your death, but you are here. You are alive, and you are rare and powerful. Strong and beautiful."

He looks to me, but these words of affection are more than I have heard in all my years of growing up. I tremble, wishing to hold him, but my full embrace would only kill him quicker. The poison in my veins, on my skin, I feel it has only grown fiercer since my death.

"Do you love me, Father? Do you truly love Beatrice the daughter and not just Beatrice the botanic creation?"

A wounded look crosses over in those dark irises. "Beatrice," he says, his voice a mere sigh. He grips my hand tighter, tries to say something else. Only a whisper emerges, and I cannot hear what drifts from those dry lips. His head falls back, resting on the thick evergreen shrub behind us, and his grip becomes loose in my hand.

I watch him die, watch him leave me, with nothing but sadness where my heart should be beating. An ache of torment roils my soul, if I have one.

Distressed and abandoned, will I never hear words of love from anyone?

The great Signor Dr. Rappaccini is no more.

I cannot deny, this is not the ending I wanted for him. For any of them. There is satisfaction, though, at bestowing some of my pain onto the three who controlled me. The father who played creator. The professor who delivered unwanted judgment. And of course, the closest I might ever know to love, to friendship—*Oh, Giovanni, you could have stayed with me for an eternity.*

Instead, my eternity is here within the garden. I move slowly toward her, my other half.

"Sister," I say to her. "Perhaps you are the only one I have loved truly, who has loved me so truly, too."

This stunning plant with her unusual gems, whom I have shared breath with. Shared heartache and embraces. "Sister, he is gone. I shall have no closure. I thought the need for closure was what brought me back, but now I know nothing."

The winds of evening twilight float through the garden, creating a whirlwind of sweet scents and loose petals.

"What do we do," I ask the wind, "when we cannot have the closure that has been driving our actions? Our very purpose?"

A delicate voice buds into the breeze, and I know it must be her. The whole garden shivers around me, speaking. My garden gods, statues and vines, emerald leaves and dirt-smeared flowers, how they chatter.

We move on, the whispers say. *We learn new blooms.*

As if possessed, I dance among the plants and shrubs. A fiery foliage takes hold of my limbs, and we spin there in the garden. It is, perhaps, the closest thing to happiness.

Maybe this is the freedom of acceptance. I am different, something born and then created, shaped. There is relief in acceptance, in knowing my future might not be the one of fairy tales and love, but my father has created something here in the garden. Striking and strange, promises blooming all around.

New strength takes me over, and I drag my poor father's body from the stone bench. He'd grown so frail that it brings about new aches in me—the vicious cycle of a human life. Like the plants I beheld since childhood, watching new sprouts bud, tiny tendrils reaching ever higher and stronger. Blooming bright at the height of life. Many of them lived for so long, even the strange, swirled hybrids Father created. Others fell, overtaken by weather or illness. Some did not survive the experiments.

To wither and shrink, to return to soil.

I return the great Signor Giacomo Rappaccini to the earth he treasured. To his beloved, poisonous Eden.

"Rest now, Rappaccini. Rest."

I breathe in the air of this place, taken by the glistening shine of it all, and I smile. A true smile. When was the last time I did that?

As the sun tucks itself into the darkening landscape, I retreat from the garden and back to my father's study. His journal is already waiting for me on the desk, turned to a blank page. Next to the journal, a bundle of pages is carefully stacked and tied with a ribbon. A quick glance at the first page sends an electric bolt through my ribs.

These are the entries about me. My birth, my childhood, my growth. My sister-plant. Everything I begged to know.

His final gift.

Not quite ready to lose myself in those pages, I trace a finger down the journal's leather spine, and this book does not burn or wince at my touch; it is strong, made for me. Not alive, so I cannot kill it, yet the leather and the paper sing for me. We are connected.

I pick up my father's writing quill:

> *Only a month after his daughter's death, Signor Rappaccini succumbed to his own fate and has been returned to the earth.*

I am his daughter, pushed up from the soil to achieve something great. Going forward, the entries on the botanical garden and future experiments will be inscribed by my hand.

—The Journal of Beatrice Rappaccini

CYANIDE CONSTELLATIONS

In the daylight, I pretend nothing can hurt me, but we both know that has never been true. What hides in shadow or creeps through the night must exist during dewy mornings and August afternoons.

I stretch my limbs beneath the buttery warmth of late summer sun, using the dirt of our never-planted garden as my bed. Heat penetrates defenseless skin, burning flesh with strips of red along my arms and legs where the dress you loved offers no protection. I should go inside, keep the lights off and hide within the cool darkness of air conditioning, but here I remain, glued to the soil as if the sun melted my body into gooey strips, pinned down like butterfly wings mounted on a board, my brittle body to be sold as art. Who would buy the art of me if there is no you?

And you are what I think about as I burn. The clay of your bones and how they formed a strong, beautiful structure. The smooth bark of your skin, like a pale aspen that grew away from the rest of its colony and learned to walk, to escape the root system where you would have stayed your whole life. Your eyes wild, unnamed blossoms, and your marrow comprised only of clouds. How the entire planet existed within the space of you.

Or maybe you consisted of constellations—the afterbirth of a galaxy that slid down from a viscous womb and tore the cosmos in two, only to land on Earth and find me. Love me. Leave me. I don't know if you returned to whatever you were before your gloom slithered into my gut, or if you're simply gone, but I so deeply wish to share my darkness with you again.

Every atom of mine aches for your blood, the salted metal of it staining my tongue. The way we entangled limbs near the river where we fantasized about drowning ourselves, about drowning others. All those times you prodded at the black fuzz of my thoughts, daring to venture a little deeper to understand how far the sickness lingered in both our souls. If you were sent here to learn about human beings, to understand them, then you never should have been sent to me.

Would you do it? you had asked once. *Would you kill her?*

One single pause as river fish swam away from the rock we lingered on, breaking the smooth water's surface into ripples. Frogs croaked between the reeds where gray snakes slid, hungry. Muddy scales blended seamlessly into the bank as they danced ever closer to their prey.

I would.

I did. Long after you dissolved back into the particles of the universe, long after my mother disappeared and my dad went to prison, I took Clara down to the river where red clay tinted the banks like rust. She asked so many times when our parents were coming home. I told her lies, told her the truth, but neither mattered. Our parents had been good to her, rotten to me, and toxic to each other. After her final round of questioning, I pressed her small head beneath the calm surface until she never moved again. All of her blonde curls soaked through until strands tangled together, forming a noose around her neck. She barely struggled.

What an amazing thing to have had her trust; the way I held it like a glass ornament in my hands and squeezed until it shattered. Such fascination electrocuted my mind when the shards cut into my palm, drew out beads of blood. I was so busy always examining my own pain, I never noticed when she suffered. At least, not until I dragged her body home, finally realized how much she'd put her faith in me.

Even then, I didn't feel a thing other than a buzzing relief that with Clara gone, they were all finally gone. *Poof,* no more life. The whole family. Freedom ricocheted through my bones with a tinny melody. The orchestra of my skeleton played on, but I had more work to finish.

You weren't here for me to tell you that I felt nothing. I let the void grow, lolled against the dirt the way a mangy dog might rub a deer carcass in the grass. Fleas and bacteria and decomposition juices soaking into the fur.

With everything and everyone gone, I can finally be gone, too. At last, I sit up and eye the prizes I brought with me into the yard.

Alone beneath the sky, where afternoon clouds transform into pink, coppery puffs of an oncoming sherbet sunset.

Alone where no one can spy because the woods offer a final divider of defense between me and the rest of the world.

Alone in the yard where I buried my sister's bloated body. I would have scattered your ashes here, too, but you left no corpse behind. Instead, I burned all the letters you wrote me before we knew how to talk about our nightmares aloud. Charred ruins of your graceful handwriting remain strewn between unkempt hedges and wild vines climbing the house, all the way to the roof where you told me your fantasy about pushing someone from a high cliff just to watch them fall. To see what the end result looked like. If the blood would spread the way it did in movies, if the brain matter would explode like a dropped watermelon on concrete.

All those perverse little questions and pleasures, how our spines quivered when we morphed our sticky thoughts into spoken words.

I would have buried my mother here, but they never found anything more than her severed hand, and my father never told them where to look for the rest. When I asked for the hand to bury it, my request came back denied since it was still seized as evidence. All I could inter was the heirloom necklace she gave me once after years of her acid words. I should have broken the thing, hammered it down until the opal softened into dust. But I treasured it. Wanted it to be a token of love and not just an apology for years devoid of affection.

At last, I come to join you all. I cannot bury myself, but there is another way. You taught me to plant my body deep within the ground, though when you whispered interstellar secrets into my ear, I knew you never expected I would be the one to carry them out.

My prizes, my scavenger hunt for death. All the things you warned me about. All the things I should never lust after, should never place upon my tongue and hold them there, daring my throat to swallow, but I can't resist. Running my fingertips over each surface, feeling the difference between smooth and jagged on the different pieces, it all sends electric jolts through my nerves. I spark like lightning, remembering the first time we touched and your skin fizzled. How I made you glow electric blue all over, learning everything that comprised your impossible body. How well we fit together, and how you could have burnt me to a cinder with your power, but you never did.

Is that what took you in the end? You never let go, never lost control, and I wonder if it all became too much and swallowed you up. Am I the reason for your absence? Did I make you hold all that raw power within your shaking cavern of a body until you collapsed back in on yourself, returning to a vast universe in the cosmos?

No matter. I will understand everything soon. I will find you, or I will find you out.

You told me so many times not to eat watermelon seeds and to avoid the bitter pits of cherries and plums. Things we learn from childhood, the edible and inedible bits of a fruit, but you were fervent with your warnings in a way that planted sour curiosity to curdle in my brain. Your entreaties against the amygdalin hidden within the center of apricots, peaches, and nectarines float away on the breeze, no longer needed. Take your warnings to the grave where they never buried your body, because I don't want them. There is no point to cautionary tales when everything else is gone.

Small seeds first, pinprick tickles as they slide down my throat with the help of gulps of water. What I cannot swallow whole, or what is too teeth-cracking to masticate, I cut in half or pummel down into chipped bites. Fragmented shards stick in my gums and between molars. Piercing slivers slash inside my cheeks, inviting blood to trickle across tongue and down my throat, where more splinters scratch.

In my grief, I defy you. What a strange thing it is to be haunted by pale memories of your strawberry mouth, your voice like birdsong, and the dark curls of eyelashes powdered with stardust. No bounty or blue jays here, though. No Orion or Ursa Major. Just me, hunching over the wooden-like insides of the fruits, their juicy flesh long gone, because it would do me no good, not with this mission. This need to understand where you went. Is Clara with you? What about my mother?

Your voice in my head ringing like a death knell, asking too many questions. *Do you regret what you did? To Clara?*

Yes, oh yes, oh yes. My baby sister, all gone.

I swallow the unpleasant teardrops of apple seeds and broken up nectarine pits. Acids release from my digestive system, turning amygdalin to cyanide, poisoning me from the inside—a place I cannot reach, a place you cannot reach me, either.

A place Clara will never grow up and understand, because I drowned her in the river and never thought about the heartbreak of that until now, right now, and now is too late. Now is nothing. The sum of all I am boils down into hunks of meat and bone, infected by regret. A toxin-filled shell of person chasing a swan song, the end to all endings before the universe you abandoned splits at the sutured veins, bursting into malleable magma rivers where minerals and rocks drip blood.

I'd tell her I'm sorry, but my mouth is full of sour venom, and time is running out. I allow no room for error. Even if my body tries to pass the poison, I will never stop in my consumption. The pulverized cherry pits, saved for last. I've mashed real cherries in with the obliterated centers, an attempt to make the taste more palatable. After all, if everything turns to bile, spills from my lips in a vomit waterfall, then my work is done for nothing. I cannot fail.

After the toxins take me and I collapse, dying from the toes up, I fall into glittering darkness. You're so close. Every jewel in the sky becomes you, inviting me to reach upward and join you in the garden of constellations where you've replanted yourself. I ache and stretch, willing my mass to ascend into the open embrace of night sky, but I am rooted here.

I am awake, aware, feeling the unexpected elation of strength and life. A lightness takes hold of my consciousness that I have never experienced before, and I only wish I could reach you.

The first vine shoots from my wrist, pushing through membrane where veins should be, but no pale blue reflects beneath it, or at least beneath whatever has replaced my skin. Transparent green encases my skeleton. Blood morphs to dirt, and bones warp into thick stalks. From within me, the seeds grow. Splintered pits nestle deep into the soil of my dead flesh and take root. Apple trees and nectarines, wild watermelon vines reach up where the cherries try to regrow from the stems of my arms. Saplings shred through the elbow crooks like flags claiming land.

All these newborn twigs sprouting from my ears, leaves spilling from my mouth, all the fruits combining together, so lovely; their cyanide churning from my stomach to give us all life again, but will it bring you back to me? My flowered sight stares at the heavens where your starry garden grows opposite of mine on Earth.

The air fills with electric scent, cold metal and lavender, like the oil you dabbed behind your ears at night. Perhaps this is our ending, to rotate around the planet—you with your constellation garden, and me splitting apart as all the toxic seeds I ingested regrow from a new body. Never quite within reach of one another. The way I will flourish during the day, only catching glimpses of you during clear nights before I sleep.

Is Clara with you? Tell her I'm sorry. Tell her I bet she's the brightest star in the sky.

I want to stare at you forever, but the tulips of my eyes tuck themselves in for the night, forcing the petals to close. The last moment I capture—a shooting star races across the obsidian sky, burning out its brightness.

WITH RADIUM ON HER LIPS

Radium. Perhaps Violet was crazy for seeking it out, but any trepidation she might have felt had died along with Sophie three months ago. She'd hoped to retrieve the chemicals sooner, but after more girls sickened and the trials progressed over U.S. Radium factories, gaining access to the substance's waste proved to be a challenge.

Her powers had weakened after Sophie's passing, but determination these past few weeks aided in strengthening Violet, both in willpower and in command over what brewed within her blood. Some sick part of her heart beat in a grateful rhythm that Sophie was walled up in a small mausoleum instead of buried underground. She'd never met Sophie's family before, and now they'd remember her as the young woman at the funeral who had too many breakdowns and left early. A good friend, a roommate whose name they heard mentioned now and then. If they suspected something more had occurred between the two women, no one would have dared utter the words aloud.

She knew how to hide. After all, she'd cloaked her magic and her love away from people for years. Sophie changed so much of that, but skulking in the shadows of a graveyard while carrying a bucket filled with radium-laced paint barely phased Violet.

She'd met Sophie inside a glittering speakeasy that was concealed behind an ivy-clad building in the West Village, about an hour from her apartment in New Jersey. The joint stood only a block away from where the feds had padlocked and shut down another bar only a week before. The new place was owned by a woman who, like Violet, knew how to hide. The tiny sprinkle of glamour made the pub difficult to find for those who contained no power within their blood, but it called to Violet the moment she walked past that ivy.

Inside, hand-painted art spread from the walls, reaching up to a sparkling ceiling that reflected kaleidoscopic colors across the tabletops and stone floors. Laughter echoed from each corner every night as patrons danced and clinked fine glasses of Bathtub Gin and Devil's Candy. The atmosphere thickened with smoke, leaving behind a feeling that nothing could penetrate these walls. No raids could stop the party; the party simply packed up and moved if the feds came. Violet remembered feeling safe those nights. These people—her people—came because they felt the tug of magic; they understood themselves to be a little different, but in here they were just normal.

Sophie had been sitting alone in a leather booth with a dark green drink. Violet locked eyes with her and then sat across from the lonely figure with loose curls and dark lipstick. When Sophie gave her a heartbreakingly beautiful smile, Violet knew she wanted to make this woman smile forever.

But forever never came. They lived together in Violet's small apartment for two years before Sophie took the job at the factory painting dials so the soldiers could have luminous watches. By the third year of their life together,

Sophie was dead. So many signs presented themselves before Sophie got achingly sick, but she never worried, never seemed to overthink the process of dipping the fine camel-hair brushes into radium paint, using her lips to point the brush over and over… It's what all the girls did, because that's how they were instructed. They'd even have parties and paint each other's nails and faces with the glowing paint. One time, Sophie had come home with her teeth painted in the strange gloop.

"It's fine," they'd all say and giggle. "The men told us it was healthy."

Those men… Violet shivered with rage as she stood outside of Sophie's vault, prepared to do something that could make other witches exile her forever. The factory owners would pay, but Violet's first priority was Sophie. It would always be Sophie.

Necromancy was a nasty, tricky art. Something Violet never intended on attempting at any point in her life. The darkness lingering in its labyrinthine magic scared her. She'd always insisted on using her power for good, for the light. To make things better. But there was no better without Sophie.

She'd broken into the mausoleum last month to prepare and left items stashed away behind loose stones along the walls. The locked gate on the door unlocked easily with help from the two pins she carried. Violet set the paint buckets aside and shoved the stones away to reveal where she'd hidden clothed bundles of materials. She rummaged for the seven candles first, lit them, and set each one around where she'd draw her circle. A breeze howled outside, and the damp tomb allowed in much of the chill. The candles flickered but held their small flames.

Violet searched for the chalk and used the white nub to trace a familiar circle on the ground. She etched drawings for protection and for empowerment. A nagging voice rooted in her brain reminded her that she could accidentally summon a demon and not conjure Sophie's soul at all. She swallowed the fear down into the sticky, cobweb basement of her stomach. Would a demonic-entity version of Sophie be that much worse than what the radium had done to her?

Anemia came first, and then the bone fractures. Sophie wore her pain on her face and had never tried to hide it. Everything Violet witnessed Sophie go through only fueled her to go through with the spell. As she completed the circle, she remembered the blood dripping from Sophie's gums, the bone tumors protruding from her jaw and distorting her face.

How terribly cruel that the thing responsible for Sophie's death would be used to bring her back, but dark magic contained strange bargains.

She didn't wish to use her power and tire out too quickly, she needed extra strength to open the heavy casket, but all the strength in the world wouldn't prepare her to see Sophie's decomposing body for the first time. She held her breath, closed her eyes, and centered her being. Words flowed through her blood and then whispered from her lips, an incantation for borrowed strength. From the earth, she pulled—connecting her body to rocks and roots—and as she took the strength to open the casket, a small boulder outside near the graveyard entrance crumbled into dust. Magic always held a price, and what she planned to do to bring Sophie back would be no exception.

The casket lid cracked and slid to the ground with an echoing clang. Violet did not move from the circle. She had no need to see the corpse. The pungent odor of rot and mildew encircling the mausoleum was enough. Choking back tears and trying not to gag, Violet focused on recentering her power.

"Come on," she whispered aloud, urging herself to work quickly, but this matter was so very delicate.

From the bag she'd stashed behind the stones, she pulled out a faded blue scarf that'd been a favorite of Sophie's. She wrapped the soft material around her neck; it was meant to keep her grounded and connected to the person she intended to raise, like a not-so-morbid memento mori. The scarf carried a hint of Sophie's perfume, but the lavender scent mixed with the stench of death only made the tomb more like a funeral home.

She placed the rest of the items in front of where she sat cross-legged in the circle: a piece of unleavened, black bread to symbolize decay; a sharp dagger encrusted with a ruby in its handle (a gift from her departed grandmother who also practiced magic, something that Violet's mother did not share); and then of course, the stolen radium paint.

The spell looked deceptively simple, but Violet could be here for hours, and she knew she might not leave alive. Or worse, that Sophie could come back so very wrong.

Deep breaths of pungent air filled her lungs. She chanted memorized words that she'd spent the past month learning by heart, phrases that twisted together Latin and what she could only understand to be the language of spirits. Her lips continued to move as she grabbed the dagger, rolled up her sleeve, and slashed into the meat of her forearm. Blood jeweled down and splattered onto the blackened bread. Violet tore off a chunk and chewed the putrefied, bloodied thing into a pulp before swallowing.

She dipped her fingers into the radium paint and drew an altar on her arm over the bleeding wound. To the spirit now whispering in her thoughts, she became the altar itself and offered these things, these pieces of life and death in exchange for Sophie.

Within Violet's head, the demon raged. Every bone in her body turned to fire, burning her from the inside out.

"What do you ssseeek?" it whispered.

"Sophie," Violet cried through the searing torment as her skin bubbled, yet she did not move out of the circle. "Her soul, back in her body." Every word became torture to speak. She told herself it wasn't real, that her melting skin was an illusion placed by the perverse creature, but the pain remained undeniable.

"What do you offer?"

"My blood." Her tongue disintegrated, and ash clogged her throat. She willed visions of the bargain into her mind's eye, an effort to show the demon what she proposed since she could no longer speak.

While popular belief held onto the notion that rituals needed a sacrifice, that was not always the case. Blood magic needn't take the life of another, and Violet could never harm anyone or any animal for her own benefit, but when it came to her own blood, she'd give it all up for Sophie.

Her body blistered from the demon's torture, but she showed it her willingness to trade her blood in order to bring her lover back. Together, they would share bodies fueled on radium paint in place of blood. Together, they would take the very toxin that killed Sophie and will it to give them life instead. The demon calmed, and from where it spoke inside her head, Violet felt the creature ripple with intrigue. The spirit world accepted her proposal.

"You are sssure?"

"Yes."

It did not ask again. A tornado of shadow descended, lifting up Sophie's rotted carcass until the bones danced with the darkness. Shadows brought forth the skeleton, mashing its body against Violet's. A curtain of night fell over Violet's eyes, and the radium-laden paint washed over her skin as the demon drained her blood. New flesh wrapped around Sophie's bones, replacing liquefied parts with shimmering meat.

Made of radium and shadow, devoid of blood, Violet knew they could never return to society. They would terrify anyone who dared glimpse them. The darkness fell away, and in its place stood Sophie, reborn. Violet bent over, gasped for air. The incantation reduced her strength to mere embers, but there she was. Her Sophie.

Her naked body glowed from the radium in her veins coursing through nearly translucent skin. If she stared hard enough, Violet could see the outline of gleaming ribs and luminescent organs. She held her own hand up and saw the same—how they both glistened like stars through a night sky. Hair disintegrated and left them both bald. Violet's own clothes hung from her body in tattered ruins. She unwound the scarf from her neck and, despite its new holes from the burn of the radium's strength, offered it to Sophie.

When she smiled and took the scarf, any lingering feeling of regret melted from Violet's mind. It was the same smile Sophie gave her their first night in the enchanted speakeasy, where incantations drifted from people's lips just as sweetly as the honeyed booze they drank. Excitement snaked through Violet's chest; they were fearsome, yes, but beautiful. It'd been a dangerous venture, to fill bodies with shadows and radium, to bargain with ancient, unpredictable spirits. A small terror lingered in Violet's thoughts, knowing now what a lonely heart was capable of. Sophie returned, though, and together they would leave this place and its torment behind.

"How?" Sophie whispered. She examined her glowing hands, ran fingertips over her smooth scalp before she rushed to Violet, kissed her. Radium lips met and sparked, igniting the mausoleum's darkness with lightning.

"We have to go." Violet reluctantly pulled away from Sophie's embrace. "I'll explain everything later. We can start a new life where no one will find us. Far away in the woods. Together."

Sophie laced her fingers with Violet's and nodded, but something sparked in those bright eyes. "Are they still alive?"

"The other girls from the factory? Some, yes, but a few more are sick. Others have died."

Sophie's lips pulled down into a stern frown. "No, the factory owners."

"Oh, yes, they're fine," Violet said, exasperation filled her at the mere thought of just how fine and unbothered those men were. Would they even be convicted? How many other girls had to die first?

Sophie seemed to share Violet's thoughts, because she tightened her grip and didn't blink as she stared into Violet's eyes. If their eyebrows hadn't fallen off, Violet knew Sophie's would be knitted together right now, determined with a plan.

"We have to take care of them first, and then we'll leave."

"Sophie, I'm exhausted. This took everything out of me. And I can't... I can't kill anyone."

"You won't have to. Besides, I feel strong." She held up the hand that wasn't clasping Violet's. Green knuckle bones gleamed through the skin. "I have to do this."

When Sophie was resolute, nothing stopped her. Violet sighed but nodded, willing to follow her anywhere. She gathered up the leftover materials and erased the chalk circle, but nothing would hide the cracked casket, the stains of the radium, or the blood drying on stone.

Dawn arrived an hour later, and Violet instantly missed the cover of darkness. Careful not to be spotted, she followed Sophie to a rented building where the men Sophie hunted often conducted their business. With the factory temporarily shut down, this was the most likely place to find the managers.

"I don't know how much help I can be," Violet said. "I'm depleted." The magic took so much, but as she looked at Sophie, she knew it gave so much, too.

"It's okay, Vi. Let me do this, and then let me take care of you for once."

It didn't take long for the three managers to arrive in the morning. Violet remained motionless from the storage closet where she hid with Sophie, watching the men from a crack between the door. She recognized Mr. Raymond from his appearances in the newspaper, and Mr. Bell from Sophie pointing him out in town once.

"Who's the other guy?" she whispered.

"Charles, maybe. He wasn't at the factory much." Sophie didn't move, so Violet followed her lead, not quite sure what the whole plan involved. Mostly, her body ached to rest.

These were the three who commanded dozens of women to use their lips to point the brushes, who promised radium was good for the girls. The three who were responsible for Sophie's death, for the deaths and sicknesses of others. Violet clenched her shining hands into fists and tried to stop shaking.

Her anger only increased when the men gathered around the table with their coffee and started discussing ways to discredit the girls going on trial.

"They're filthy liars."

"Fools."

"Tell the judge they all have syphilis."

The men chuckled, and Sophie screamed. She burst through the storage closet, and as the men gaped at her, Violet stumbled to the only door and locked it. She planted herself there as a guard, but if the men came at her, she hadn't the strength to fend them off. It took all she had to simply stand up straight and not collapse onto the floor.

For about three seconds, the men just stared, and then chaos erupted. Maybe-Charles cowered in a corner, Mr. Raymond stood paralyzed, and Mr. Bell eyed the door. Every atom in Violet's body screamed to sleep, but she held her ground. She hoped the urgency in her eyes encouraged Sophie to hurry.

Bell dashed for the door, but Sophie grabbed his wrist. The toxins in their bodies that now kept them alive were like radium dialed up to a thousand for others. Sophie's touch seared through Bell's wrist, melting flesh down to sinew and bone. Charred meat stunk up the room as the man howled and fell backward.

"If you don't want that to happen to all of you, then shut up and listen," Sophie said. She took a step closer, and Raymond fumbled in his pocket only to bring out a small knife. Bell rocked on the floor, nursing his scorched skin.

"What's wrong, Mr. Bell, don't recognize me? You said I was your favorite worker. What about you, Mr. Raymond? How many times did you try to grab all the girls by the skirt as we left at night?"

Nausea churned in Violet's gut. "I didn't know that," she whispered.

Sophie turned toward her and offered a sad smile. "From what some of the girls told me, he's done worse."

"Lies! Those girls came on to me. Who are you, a freak?" Raymond's words might have been laced with anger, but the stuttering fear in every vowel rang out loud and clear to Violet. She watched as rage flashed in Sophie's eyes before she calmly walked over to Raymond and placed a hand across his cheek.

He screeched worse than a wounded animal as his cheek burned. Flesh melted into stringy bits, dangling from his jaw and burning a hole clean through until his teeth were visible from the outside.

"You should have seen what the radium did to my face," Sophie said. "I guess this is close enough."

She walked over to where their coffee still sat in big white mugs. "These jokers are pathetic."

"Sophie…" Violet heard her own voice fading. Gray spots clouded her vision.

"One more second. Then we're outta here." Sophie grabbed the pocketknife Raymond dropped. She made a clean slash across her arm and drained oozing radium from her body into each cup.

"You taught me so much Vi; I hope this works." She smiled and closed her eyes, familiar words chanted from radiant blue lips. A charm to command the actions of others… Violet had never used it herself, but it was written out in her favorite spellbook from her grandmother. Apparently, Sophie had been studying more than Violet realized back then.

"Drink your coffee, gents."

Sophie's glow paled, and Violet recognized weariness from the magic. They put their arms around each other's waists, lending strength. In a trance, the men moved toward the radium-laced coffee.

Mr. Bell grabbed his mug with the wrist that still bore flesh, and some of the liquid spilled from the hole in Mr. Raymond's cheek. The third man gulped his coffee down between screams as the powerful toxin worked its way from the inside, sickening and poisoning them, just like their dangerous lies had infected the girls at the factory. But this, Violet knew as she cast one last glance before disappearing down the hall with Sophie, this was a hundred times quicker and a hundred times more painful.

Sophie kissed her cheek, and Violet smiled, but she halted in her walk as her mind raced.

"Vi?" Sophie tilted her head.

Violet leaned forward and crashed her lips against Sophie's, pressing her body against the wallpapered hall. The paper singed and smoke drifted from beneath Sophie's naked back, but the kiss sparked through Violet, reviving her power for long enough to do one final thing.

"Wow," Sophie whispered, dazed and smiling. Violet rushed back into the office before the borrowed charge left her. She locked eyes with one of the men still under the trance, not yet dead. A spark of power laced with radium danced up Violet's throat and spilled from her lips in a whisper that traveled to the man's ear.

"Pick up the knife," she said and pointed to where it rested on the table. "Cut your arm. Leave a message in blood and warn the world about radium, about the factories, about everything the girls went through. Spill it all."

He nodded and picked up the knife.

The world might take some time to learn everything, Violet knew, but as she went back into the hall and laced her hand with Sophie's, she had everything she needed. Together, they were radium girls wandering through a strange world, but their glowing bodies and iridescent incantations would light their way no matter where they went.

AVIAN EYES

The birds leave, and the birds return.

I always wait, watching the horizon for V-shaped figures to crest over the hill and fly down to the pond we share. This area was here long before I purchased the property, and I have the feeling it will remain long past my inevitable death.

For the past three months, I've spent every night watching the moon. I wonder how the birds are doing up there and if they've turned a crater into a nest. I don't know what they eat, but they usually return looking healthy, though hungry. There's so much humankind doesn't know, but the birds know. They've learned to adapt, to fly through stars and time with wings stretched wide. Magic resides within these avian creatures, and I can't seem to draw myself away. I've never wanted to.

When March breaks open with buttery dawn, the birds return at last. I tidy the wooden houses, fill the feeders, clean out the stone fountain by the pond's side. A thin creek connects the pond to a brook in the woods, and I spend some time removing twigs and black walnuts from the water source. Everything will be perfect. When the weather warms, large-leaved lupines will sprout with bursts of purple along the stream, luring insects and other life. It's a kind of enchantment, to be a part of and watch the transformation of the seasons.

Cold seeps through my jeans as I sit on rocks, remembering when I first met the blue jays years ago. So stubborn, but they warmed to me when I brought suet and sunflower seeds. Male cardinals came next, brilliant as rubies. Cracked corn lured in blackbirds and a few brave squirrels from the surrounding forest.

I learned to trade trinkets with the crows, exchanging peanuts for keys, lost earrings, and bones. Where did they find these objects? Deep in the woods, or did they pluck some items from unsuspecting people in town? I don't care much for the townspeople. When I speak to them of the great moon migration, they look at me as if I've sprouted an extra head.

Ravens, perhaps like my fellow humans, were trickier when it came to earning trust. Clever things. They couldn't resist the treat puzzles, though. Always eager to prove themselves and their wit. As for the owls, I stayed out of the way as they fetched fish from the pond or mice in the fields. Trust, beautiful and delicate, spun a thread from the birds to me. I've been here for seven winters, and each spring fills me with the same spark of excitement.

The birds swoop down from the sky and encircle the pond, which also encircles me. They've never descended like this, forming a rigid circle of robins, blackbirds, grackles, loons, and all the others I've met before. They have returned from their moon migration, but tension spoils the homecoming. What's changed?

I glance into those eyes I cherish. Sharp and aware, black, amber, others with blue irises or red. Those once innocent eyes glower, altered. Something like knowledge, the terrible power of it, reflects back.

"What's wrong?" I ask the birds. Lunar aroma puffs from their plumage—that strange scent like fresh gunpowder. A starling shakes bits of moon dirt from glossy wings.

What did the moon teach them?

They're willing me to understand what I cannot. All of their individual irises, the whole rainbow spectrum, transform into glowing beads of teal. I gaze at them, and a word appears unwanted in my mind:

Drink.

Garbled birdsong emits from throats and beaks. In the circle's center, the owls rise. One carries a limp, crimson body, and places the dying cardinal at my feet. I kneel to reach out a hand to the poor creature, but another owl shreds my skin while its companion slashes a talon across the cardinal's throat.

He bleeds, and there's that word again.

Drink.

They swarm. Talons hold me in place as the owl picks up the red body. Others yank my hair, pull my head back. Feathers against my lips, reeking of death and ozone. Liquid oozes in, slides down my throat like a paste of rotten raspberries. Lukewarm and sour.

I drink until there is no more, until I am collectively freed by these moon-changed birds. Chin and mouth slicked with blood, I clutch at the hard earth, visions of stars burning cold in my skull. My skin stretches, and the air sprouts metallic blooms.

Owls hoot, and ravens give gurgling croaks. Slow vibrations from the others rattle my nervous system as my eyesight blasts with ultraviolet colors.

Avian vision. I weep at such a spectacular gift.

"Is this what you learned to do on the moon?"

The birds trill, their song deep and steady. Speckles of lunar dust glow like uranium on their feathers and from within me. I am burning ember blue as I stumble up. Pores bleed from pinfeathers spiking out of flesh. My toes lengthen. New bones ache.

A different language slots itself together in my memories, warbling as I listen.

Give the humans wings. Feathers.

Let them rip one another to shreds in the clouds if they refuse our future.

We will keep her.

I am theirs, so they tell me. The first. Not their Eve, but their Lilith. A way forward in the remaking of nature. Bestowed transformation, so that I may also reward it in return. Do they deserve it, though, all of those people who laughed at me?

Give them no choice, the robins sing.

The birds leave, and the birds return. This time, they have returned especially for me. Will I be able to migrate with them to the moon next winter? My spine ablaze, I have no wings yet, but something spreads there, pushing around the skin. Making room.

Our blood together, fused with lunar dust and cosmic debris. My world is already remade, glowing bright within avian eyes. I stretch and trill, eager to share this gift with humankind.

MOONFLOWERS

Splatters of orange spread across the evening sky like melting globs of ice cream. Gwen Hallie turned her head away from the faded colors as the world darkened. The last light of a dying sunset caught her red hair in a blaze before the sun disappeared behind the distant hills. Bright stars crept out into the evening and glittered across the atmosphere.

Gwen's own eyes concentrated on the flowers that swayed in the wind five feet from where she sat. She crawled across the field, inching closer to the blooms. Dirt clung to her black dress and stuck to her palms. Wind rustled through the trees and carried the swirled aroma of florae. What strange little blossoms the wildflowers were, curved like a flattened star with white petals that only opened for a nocturnal embrace.

Leo had loved the moonflowers almost as much as he had loved her. He wanted to plant them in the garden, but his work at the architecture firm consumed his time like a greedy leech. He was so busy that final month of his life, so far away, trapped in his mind with all those designs and blueprints. Architectural ghosts, begging to be constructed.

Gwen sighed and traced her fingertips through the cool soil where the moonflowers flourished. A bare spot in the earth lay next to the blooms. The spot where Leo was buried. The moonflowers did not yet have time to reach their vines across and seal him in. Despite the mound of naked soil, the copse was a beautiful place to sleep forever.

The trees formed a crescent around the flat hilltop, and the thicket protected anything hidden inside from harsh daylight. It was the perfect spot to watch sunsets descend over the flowers Leo loved, as if forming the garden he never had time to tend. A kaleidoscope of white, blue, pink, and yellow wildflowers dotted the hill, and Gwen's heart ached at the beauty she enjoyed while her husband no longer could.

Leo's mother had found the place beautiful, too, and said she wished she could have buried Leo's father in a place like this. Her eyes had formed a haunted look, as if she was remembering again how Leo's father died, the way the aneurysm burst in his head like a crushed cherry tomato.

At least he didn't scream, Leo's mother always said, *thank God he didn't scream*. The only screaming this time had come from Fynn and his arguments with Gwen about the old family cemetery. "It's a tradition!" he had shouted.

"I'll bury my husband where I like!" she shouted back. They had been hyenas that night, circling around the thought of Leo.

Harsh lights assaulted Gwen's eyes as a vehicle crawled up the dirt road at the bottom of the hill. A black convertible came to rest in the driveway. Fynn stepped out of his car, and from here his silhouette resembled Leo's so much; Gwen had to inhale several times and bite her cheek to keep the emotional waterfall in her chest intact. The ache of loss cemented itself between her ribcage.

I wish I had your hunting knife, Leo. I would cut you out of me, like a tumor.

But the knife had been left with Fynn, and she would not ask for it back. She placed her palms against her belly, knowing what beat beneath her skin could never really be cut out.

Fynn walked toward her house and thudded his hand against the big front door. She could have called out to him, but she remained silent.

She placed her cheek against the grave's mound and inhaled the earthy scent. Her ear pressed against the dirt, as if trying to hear Leo's heart beat one more time. Her tongue darted out to collect a small sample of the soil. She held it in her mouth for a moment before swallowing. She imagined the dirt traveling down to her belly, down to where half of Leo's heart still lived inside her.

She had been worried at first, concerned that eating the dead man's heart would make her ill or give her bad karma, but she felt okay. She felt Leo was still with her, thumping inside her stomach as if regenerating.

With one last glance at the moonflowers, she stood and stretched, brushing the worst of the dirt off her dress. She grabbed the black heels she meant to wear tonight from where they were tossed on ground. Soft earth greeted her toes, and the blades of grass were filled with cricket songs.

Fynn's hands rested on his hips, and his head turned wildly toward the dark house, toward the hill, toward the distant woods. He looked less like his brother in that moment. Leo had the patience of a priest listening to confessionals. Fynn turned to the hill again. He went from hands on hips to arms across chest like a worried housewife.

"You're filthy," he said. She stepped into the heels and kept her eyes low. Fynn was tall and lean like Leo, same stubble, same chestnut hair, but these were not the things that bothered Gwen. It was the eyes. Fynn's were the same burnt brown, an absolute replica of her Leo's. She had her days where she could tolerate looking into them, but tonight was not one of them. The last time she saw Leo's eyes they had been lifeless, and his brown irises resembled that of a rotten apple's core.

Hands brushed at the bottom of her dress and across her knees at the leftovers of dirt. She stood there and stared forward. There wasn't much else to do these days.

"I'm sorry about all these fights," he said, and then wrapped warm fingers around her wrists. She withdrew from the touch.

Fynn did not reach for her again. "We both loved him. And you and I, we're family too. We shouldn't be arguing."

Part of her agreed, but she was too afraid to look into his eyes. Even before Leo died, Fynn would look at her in that unblinking way, like a child who coveted his brother's plaything.

He walked over to the passenger door and held it open. She slid into the convertible, inhaled the night air, and shut her tired eyes. They made their way down the rocky driveway. She waited to speak until she felt the turn onto smooth pavement.

"I'm sorry, too. I know you blame me, but I—"

The tires wailed in protest as the car spasmed to an unplanned stop. Gwen opened her eyes, grabbed onto her seatbelt, and turned her head toward Fynn.

"I don't," he started to say, but his voice turned to throaty bubbles. "I don't blame you. Don't ever think... Why would you even think that? It was an accident. I hope you don't blame yourself?" He jumped at the sound of a car horn behind them and started to drive again. He kept his eyes fixed on the road, and she kept her eyes fixed on him.

"Of course I blame myself. If I had been awake, I could have saved him or called an ambulance," Gwen protested. "And I'm the one who refused to have the autopsy done. I know everyone wanted to find out what happened, but it didn't seem right after what happened with your father, tearing open his skull just to see the thing that killed him. It's not natural." She paused.

"I wanted Leo to be as whole as he could be before the burial; that's why I had to do it myself. I'm sorry. I'm so sorry." The threatening rain behind her eyes slithered forth; big dewy drops tracked down her cheeks, and she tried not to make any more noises. She hated to sound like a snuffling animal, reduced to an incoherent mess because she lost her mate.

She closed her eyes again and concentrated on the warm air and the sound of wind that knocked around the convertible. She would like to be the wind, unseen and free.

The moment they arrived at the ceremony Leo's company put together, she went for the wine. Dark red. Dry. In the span of two hours, she was sure she had more wine than was socially acceptable, but who would say no to the grieving woman? She spoke to no one, only gave small smiles and hugs. People took turns speaking at the podium in front of the reserved restaurant and talked about Leo as if they really had known him.

The company's boss, West Jedson, droned on, but the warm buzz inside Gwen's head did not allow her to pay much attention. His wooly white mustache bobbed up and down as he spoke.

"...will always be missed. I want to wrap up tonight by thanking Mrs. Hallie for being as supportive of this company as her husband always was." West nodded his head in her direction and gave a weak smile. "And finally," he continued, "to commemorate Leo, we have agreed unanimously to name the newly built bridge he was such an integral part of, Moonflower Bridge. Anyone who knew Leo even a small while knew those were not only his favorite flowers, but also his favorite nickname for Mrs. Hallie."

Gwen's heart thudded and her face grew hot. She had not known what the bridge would be named. The company had just sent a letter asking her to be present at the ceremony to remember Leo. She figured it would be Leonard Bridge or some stupid shit, not something so personal.

West spoke on. "The bridge officially opens tomorrow to public transportation, and we hope Leo's spirit will watch over all who pass across the river."

Gwen did not stir from her seat as West shook a few hands, Fynn's included. Others started to leave and cast wary glimpses at her, some waved goodbye, but no one came to speak to her. They were probably afraid of upsetting the drunken widow. She snorted into her wine and finished off the glass. A few drops stuck to the bottom.

A draft of wind flowed in from the open deck doors and sent shivers across Gwen's skin. The deck's walkway led off to a pedestrian pathway across the new bridge. Visible from the glass windows was the moonlight. Its silver glow shone onto the steel structure and the rough water below. The white curtains around the door continued to quietly dance, and her shivers were replaced with tremors as a figure began to materialize in the doorway.

Her glass slipped from her grasp because there, quiet and tall between the curtains, stood her Leo. The glass shattered into misshapen fragments coated in the last drops of crimson wine. The shards crunched beneath her heels as she walked over to the door.

Voices attempted to enter her mind, but they were far away and dimmed. Someone may have called her name, but she only cared about Leo. He was there and she was here, and she must find him again.

Her flesh grew hot as dizziness spun into her mind. Every nerve trembled like plucked harp strings as she stumbled along. She rushed out the door and across the cobbled pathway that connected the restaurant to the new bridge. This would be it, where Leo would meet her, where he would come and take her away.

She stood alone on Moonflower Bridge and called out his name. The wind gusts turned colder. She shivered, not from the breeze, but from something deep inside her that had frozen as memories threatened to resurface. The bad memories of Leo. Of herself.

Gwen walked toward the edge of the bridge and leaned over to peer into the dark water. The river's rushing sounded like Leo, like his calm breaths and beating heart, like their names were being whispered in the rhythm of the current, *GwenLeoGwenLeo.*

If she jumped, could she drown in his words? Would her body float down along the current to him?

The water summoned her, whispered in his voice, *Jump, Gwen, and let me hold you again.*

She climbed to the bridge's ledge.

"Gwen!" Fynn ran toward her, arms outstretched. "What the hell are you doing?" The color in his face faded to a sickening paleness.

"Leo," she said into the darkness, her voice a croak. The air was so tight, so suffocating. The river called, and she yearned to shout, *I hear you! I'm coming.*

She gazed back down into the water, but fingernails dug themselves into her sides and yanked her away. Fynn's eyes were blown wide, and he breathed heavy, sweat trickled down from his temple. He looked at her and shook his head, asked a silent question that she did not have an answer for.

"Leo is gone. He's gone, but you can't be gone, too. You can't throw yourself off a bridge, for Christ's sake." Fynn leaned closer to her, ran a hand up and down her bare arm. He leaned his forehead against hers. Oh, his cologne even smelled like Leo's.

Would his heart taste like Leo's, too?

His puff of breath ghosted across her lips, and he brought his face closer. His lips began to brush against hers.

Gwen, the river whispered. *GwenLeoGwenLeo.*

She shoved Fynn away and swallowed down a scream. Her lungs ached to yell into the night, to call out to the moon and demand her old life back.

Fynn took a step toward her, but she held up a hand. "Stop." Her body shuddered.

"Gwen." Fynn reached for her.

"Is this how you show respect for your dead brother? By betraying him? You are vile," she said and only half believed her own words. There had been disgust, slick and green, swimming in her lungs for weeks now, right after Leo died. The disgust was not from anything Fynn had done, but it felt good to take it out on someone.

"I loved my brother. But he isn't here to betray anymore. Gwen, for so long I—"

"I don't want to hear it."

"I'm sorry." His words trailed off, and his eyes looked at something behind her.

She spun around. *Leo.* The figure glowed white, like an exploding star, and there was not a clear face, but the build and height were the same as Leo's. An uneven hole was visible where his heart should have been, as if a shotgun blast had blown through the ghost and left a dark void.

He held out his hand, and the light from his body pulsed.

"Gwen," Fynn uttered. "What are you doing?"

"I owe my husband an apology," she said. Her heels clicked against the bridge. Fynn hissed out more words behind her and tried to grab her arm. She kicked at his knee and ran free from the grip. Leo's figure stood on the ledge, and she hauled herself up the concrete barrier.

If this was what Leo wanted, she would make amends his way.

The ghostly figure did not speak, but the river did. Once again in her dead husband's voice it murmured to her, *Jump.*

Her skin hit the cold water with a noise somewhere between a splash and a crunch. She fought against the current that cut into her with its strength. Her body ached with bruises and possible breaks. What was she fighting against the current for? Leo came here to lull her under, to embrace her, yet she fought.

Gwen stopped her battle and gave into the cruel caress of the water. The river seeped into her mouth and ears. She had to fight the horrible strangle of suffocation, but she thought of Leo, and her panic lessened and was replaced with longing, but something went wrong. Fingernails dug into her sides, lifted her up, and as another wave of water rolled down inside her lungs, the world became cold and black.

When the darkness faded, Gwen's awareness was limited. A man spoke calm words and cradled her in his arms. He almost sounded like Leo. Her eyes opened slowly and itched from the river's gunk that left traces between her lashes. The bridge loomed above. The not-quite-Leo voice told her to hold on, to breathe, that help was on the way.

She rolled away from the arms and tumbled onto the ground. Her lungs revolted against the movement, and a large bubble of water rose up her throat. She coughed and heaved until her throat stung.

"Why did you do that?" Fynn's voice. She did not turn to face him. The whine of an ambulance's siren cried in the distance.

"Take me home," Gwen gasped, liquid sputtering from her mouth. Her coughs tasted metallic.

"What? No, you need to go to the hospital."

"If you ever want to see me again, take me home now." She leaned back to stare at Fynn with what she could only assume were red-rimmed eyes, and with a mix of water and puke drooling down her face. Her lungs burned, and her rib cage throbbed.

"I'll be fine. Please," she crawled over to him and placed a hand against his cold cheek. She coughed more, and his brow furrowed, but she pleaded again. He broke.

Fynn half carried her to the car, but she said nothing. She needed to go home, not take an ambulance ride.

She did not remember the drive or closing her eyes, but when she opened them, she was surprised to see the house in view already. Fynn walked around to open the passenger door and attempted to carry her. She held up a hand and stood. Her legs shook, and Fynn placed his palm on the small of her back. Gwen jumped away like a startled cat and zigzagged wordlessly into the house. She stumbled every few steps and glanced up where Leo rested. His figure, the glowing white one, swayed in the waning moonlight on top of the hill. It began to glide down toward the house.

From inside the kitchen with the peeling blue paint, Gwen glanced out the window. Leo's figure with its missing heart approached closer. Fynn stood with his back toward the window and did not notice the ghost. His brother.

"Is this what we're going to act like now, huh? I'm the bad guy because I care for you. Am I responsible for Leo dying in his sleep now, too?" Fynn yammered on, and Gwen wished he would stop. Stop talking, stop breathing. Just stop.

"No, no," she muttered and chanced a glimpse. She startled. The figure stood directly outside the window now. "Of course you're not responsible for Leo's death. I am." The ghost materialized through the kitchen walls. It drifted directly behind Fynn.

Gwen, it whispered to her. It whispered *inside* her mind. Leo's voice.

"He wasn't going to stay. I had to make him stay," she said. She tried to keep her eyes on Fynn, but her gaze flickered between him and the faceless apparition.

"What do you mean?"

She sighed. Leo whispered to her, but she could not discern the words. His anger toward his brother, though, and his pain at what she had done to her own husband resonated clearly. The emotions rattled her skull, and she had to take care of these problems. She must make amends.

Cut it out. Cut the tumor out.

She asked Fynn if he wanted to stay the night, to make sure she would be all right. His facial expression went from surprised, to pleased, to confused. He nodded.

"I still think we should go to the hospital," he said. "Maybe in the morning, at least."

"No, I'm fine. You can stick around for as long as you like and make sure," she said. She walked toward Leo and shivered from the cold material of her thin dress that stuck to her wet skin. Fynn turned but gave no reaction. He could not see the ghost this time.

"You have to stay," she said to Leo—the faceless Leo that was hers. Her body ached to hold him.

"Yeah, for as long as you like," Fynn said. She ignored him and instead walked over to the countertop where two glass jars waited. The glowing figure's hand hovered over them.

"Leo really loved the moonflowers," she said and slid the larger jar closer.

"Are you all right?" Fynn was at her side. His hand reached out toward her again. She turned her head and took the lid off the glass jar, pulling out a sugar cookie shaped like a moonflower.

"I made these for him, the night he died. They took forever to get into this shape. I thought it would be impossible, but I was proud of them." She handed the baked good to Fynn. He took it slowly in his hand, as if it were something precious.

She tugged at her wet hair, slime-covered from the river. The damp red strands were dark as old blood. "This is what he wanted me to be, isn't it? His adoring housewife, and I was! I *am*. But then came the bridge project, and he was always gone." She slammed her fist down on the counter, rattled the glass jars. Fynn wrapped an arm around her shoulders.

"I tried, Fynn, but it was so boring. Being stuck in this house day after day with Leo's architectural ghosts. That last night was so perfect, though. I made those," she said. "I should have died too, but I was afraid. I'm not anymore."

"What are you talking about?" Fynn stepped closer and locked his eyes to hers. She watched the dark shadow of possession travel across brown irises.

"You're not going to let me go, are you?" she said. He looked at her as she had always looked at Leo, and she told herself that made this okay, to die a lover's death.

"Try it?" She pointed to the cookie and placed her hand on his arm. There was a humming in her head, an elated sort of anticipation that emitted from Leo's ghost and into her.

"Of course." He smiled and bit into the moonflower-shaped cookie.

As Fynn chewed, she continued to talk. The hum from the ghost intensified, vibrated inside Gwen's bones. She slid the smaller glass jar closer. A strong, stinging odor clouded around the container.

"We had dinner on the deck. We stayed there until the moon was high in the sky, and he held me, and it was all I wanted—to stay in that moment forever. I gave him a cookie. He smiled and said 'moonflowers from my moonflower,' and he went to sleep there on the deck, and he didn't wake up," she said. The kitchen was smothered in silence. Fynn's hand shook, and he sat the rest of the cookie on the marble countertop. His Adam's apple bobbed as if trying to regurgitate the food.

Gwen unclasped the lid of a canopy jar next to the glass one filled with moonflower cookies. From the white container, she pulled out the other half of Leo's heart. The dried out, ragged organ was not a pretty sight from her crooked cutting of the heart, but she treasured it so.

"Do you want some water?" she asked casually.

Fynn gasped, clutched his chest, and collapsed onto the kitchen tile. Leo's faceless ghost glided out of the house and back toward the hill. Gwen kneeled near Fynn's twitching body, clutching the remains of Leo's heart. Part of her yearned to bite into it, to feel her jaw pop and work through the muscle as she had with the other half, but if she swallowed it down to join the parts inside her, would Leo's ghost disappear?

Fynn's eyes rolled back in his head as he seized from the poison. She stepped over his dying, jerking body, and went to find Leo.

Outside, she breathed in the early morning air like a familiar friend. She kicked off her heels and walked up the hill, listening to the crickets still singing songs. She knelt by Leo's grave and placed her hands on the mound of earth. The cold dirt reminded her of Leo's body when she went to it on the deck that following morning after he ate the poison she had baked. She cut out his heart and buried him herself. An architectural design all her own.

The moonflowers' blossoms began to close as the first stretch of light awoke in the sky. Beneath the flowers, where a small trickle of stream babbled, swayed the deadly water hemlock she used to bake into the cookies.

Leo's ghost hovered beside her. He began to fade as the dawn approached.

"Forgive me?" she said. Her heart thudded in rhythm to his name. *Leo. Leo. Leo.*

He placed a hand that glowed against her skin, and it was a warm, silken caress. *There's only one way,* he whispered inside her mind. *Be with me. Always.*

The masticated strings of his heart seemed to rattle within her, promising a new kind of life. She dug through the soil just enough to bury the remains of his heart and then plucked a piece of hemlock from the nearby weeds. She curled up into a tight ball on the ground and brushed the plant over her lips.

"I love you, Leo. More than anything, I love you." She rested her head on the soil over his grave, opened her mouth, and placed the small white petals against her tongue. As her mouth closed, the ghost seeped back into the earth above his grave. She chewed the sour threads of the plant slow, swallowed, and closed her eyes.

The morning sun broke over the trees, and the faint rays stretched down to the moonflowers. As the light softly touched the petals, they retracted upon themselves, protesting the intruder. The petals slowly curled in on themselves into buds as she imagined curling herself once again in Leo's arms.

ACIDIC ATONEMENT ON SULFUR PLANET

Compact dirt beneath my feet, orange-brown like rusted chains. All the colors here reflect a dying auburn, and it almost reminds me of fall and how beautiful I used to find that back on Earth, but no beauty resides here. No cascading leaves, no pumpkin patches, no hot cider waiting on the other end of a haunted maze. Rocks, dirt, volcanoes, sulfur, smoke, and acid—these are the ingredients that make up my current home.

Scientists had officially named this planet, as with all the others, after a series of letters and numbers. Codes none of us ever bother to remember. Instead, we nicknamed all the new places within reach thanks to the quick evolutions of so much technology. Some places will remain forever uninhabitable, like Wasp, a nasty exoplanet west of us that ate light. Others, scientists and astronauts could at least visit, like the Azure Planet and Super Saturn, which awaited in the north. Mega Planet, the Frozen Wasteland, Kepler, Blood Water, and probably a million others we'll never discover.

I remember reading about so many of them in the news: A planet that rained sapphires and rubies, one that rained glass during violent storms. Engineers had developed intelligent pods that could gather materials from those planets without having to be piloted by a human, which was good since sometimes the pods came back shredded and on their last ounce of artificial life.

Mars had been renamed Red Earth to make it more palatable to the colonizers, the survivors who traveled from old Earth to the new planet where humans could figure out a way to destroy that place, too. Maybe I'm too cynical and everything is going well there; I'll never know. My work here, on what we've nicknamed Sulfur Planet, will keep me planted on this sphere of rust most likely until my death. At one time, the governments promised technology would be able to take our places, but then we were deemed too unimportant. They claimed humans were needed to mine the sulfur due to such a delicate operation, but in reality, they just wanted someone to do the hard work at the cheapest price.

Before the collapse of Earth, most governments joined in a temporary solidarity to ensure the survival of life. It's amazing how much shit doesn't matter when the species is under threat of being wiped out. They asked for volunteers to do so much, jobs that sounded far over my head, but I was willing to put in the work, any kind of work. My will to live wasn't the strongest, but I also feared death; otherwise, I would have stayed on Earth and watched how it all ended, let my body disintegrate into ash with everything else. All those plants and animals, skyscrapers and highways… Nothing mattered in the end.

I had already signed up for transport to Sulfur Planet before I saw the stipend attached. More money than I'd ever seen in my life. Money that all went to my sister and her family. All of it. Thousands of dollars at my fingertips, gone. I dropped it off on her doorstep, told her to take everyone and go, and watched them depart to Red Earth. The only safe place for humans now, the only thing that would ever come close to the planet we once called home, before it spun into a sun-fried fate.

Lori had refused at first, told me she couldn't take that much money unless I departed with them, joined the family pod before it launched into space with the rest of the fleet. The desperate plea in her eyes will haunt me until my day's end. She wanted to go, and maybe that day a part of her wanted me to go with them, but I knew she'd never trust me. Not after what I did. How could I tag along with her family after I almost destroyed it?

If forgiveness was an option, I would never deserve it.

I sent them away, waited my turn to board the labor pods with my fellow workers, and I arrived on the planet of volcanoes and sulfur.

Today, I awake with the others in the cool hours of morning. Light breaks through the orange sky. It's always orange here, like a calm, fiery sea that envelopes Sulfur Planet eternally. Mornings bring soft cantaloupe shades, and the evenings turn to a dark marmalade, broken up with apricot-like hues throughout the afternoons. I leave the sleeping quarters with my backpack strapped on tight, carrying the few snacks and liquids we have available to us. On the first of each month, a supply pod arrives to replenish our stores before flying away to another destination. At least, that's what they tell us, that there are other humans on different planets doing important work. How our technology could be so evolved yet so greatly lacking at the same time, I'll never understand it. All of us separated from our families because we've been sold the idea that we're helping to ensure the survival of humanity, but what good did humanity do in the first place? Maybe we were never meant to outlast Earth's extinction.

I march quietly in line, traverse across red soil paths that lead down to the volcano field. Sulfur Planet was a baffling discovery. Despite its acid lakes and poisonous plants that thrived from the noxious nature of this world, the atmosphere was deemed suitable for careful habitation. The inability to grow food or purify water remains an issue, but the supply ship hasn't let us down yet, and the fact that we have breathable air here, my mind still can't quite process it all. Each breath feels downright crisp and clear compared to those last few years on Earth. Maybe this planet was like Earth at one point, but we landed millions of years too early, or too late.

Before arriving, I expected to have to wear the suits and bubble-like helmets that those journeying to Red Earth needed, but the atmosphere here, it's welcomed us from the beginning. It's a shame the whole planet is full of volcanoes and toxic water; otherwise, I wouldn't mind the idea of living here for the rest of my life, taking in the orange sky and walking across the foreign soil each day. But nothing will grow here, will ever thrive, except the sulfur that we mine.

Sometimes the nights unsettle me with that velvet cover of darkness. I toss and turn in my cot, fixate on fears of the volcanoes erupting, of the supply ship forgetting to stop, of other terrors I refuse to let my mind revisit as I follow my coworkers down the steep ledges and onto the rocky fields of dirt where the volcanoes wait. As I look at the others, I wonder if settling down here isn't exactly what we're doing anyway. How many of us will ever get the chance to leave?

I take care not to trip over the jutting rocks before jogging onto the flatter surfaces, lest I fall to my death. That would be tragic, but more importantly, it would slow the others down. As one of the only women working on Sulfur Planet, it has become my personal mission to never give them reason to doubt me. And so, I follow in the line where we march like ants, and I carry my wide baskets full of sulfur, collecting my fair share. Even still, I know I'm lucky we have help from artificial intelligence in collecting the full baskets, because unlike the others who have mined before on Earth, I'm not sure I could carry hundreds of pounds of the material on my shoulders. Complaints won't do any good, though. No one cares enough to listen. There's no union. There's nothing but us and the volcanoes.

And consequences. It's kind of amazing how even after the heat death of Earth, there are still men who are here to observe us, to judge us for something they view as lesser and beneath them. Men who get paid more or granted special privileges on Red Earth. If I don't meet my quota, punishment will await. We don't speak of the punishment with each other, but we know there are different levels. Maybe they take some of your pay away, maybe they beat you, or maybe you disappear like the man last month whose bones were found in one of the acid pools, melted down like a gluey substance stuck to the banks of dirt surrounding those green waters.

Guards, we call them. Medieval guards who delight in torturing those less fortunate. They change every few months, sending new men to come watch us. Some much crueler than others. Sometimes our coworkers do not return from their punishments, and until that evening when I stumbled across the bones by the acid pool, I never dared let myself think these guards would be so cruel as to throw any of us into volcanoes or toxic vats. But what other options exist out here in this lawless place?

Defenseless in terms of weapons, I sleep with sharp rocks beneath my bed. All of the women here do. We are few, but we aren't stupid. And if I had to give those horrible guards praise for anything, it would be that they aren't tolerant of any workers sneaking into the habitat where the women sleep, where sometimes men tried to slip beneath thin sheets, uninvited.

The guards were ruthless, yes, but they favored productivity, and if someone was found to be interrupting the precious sleep of another worker at night, well, we never saw those men again, either. It hurt that our fellow workers would try to use us so, but I like to tell myself the bones I found that day were of someone who deserved to have their skin melted off by acid. Someone who had tried to hurt the woman who slept near me at night—she never spoke, never told anyone her name, but she screamed that night when a man had hovered above her. The guards dragged him away, and then it was his turn to scream. He never came back.

All of this desperation, these terrible prices to pay just for the opportunity to live. But what kind of life is this to so many of the people here? Surely, they couldn't have all volunteered to come to redress their sins like I have.

I'm not fooling myself during any of this process. None of these days could fool me. If any of the others dared look me in the eye one day and ask, "Cora, did you come here to punish yourself?" I would answer yes in unflinching honesty. Yes, of course. How could I ever have come here if I wasn't on some road to atonement?

For as long as I can recall, people have told me to apologize for any wrongdoing because it's the honest, right thing to do. That's all bullshit. Apologies and confessions, they only help to relieve our guilt and pass the burden onto another. When I told my sister what I did, it felt good at first to have someone to share my darkness with, to finally make her see how messed up I was, but it all made her hate me. And then she hated herself because, forever my big sister, she cleaned up the mess I left behind. I ruined her life when I could have lied, protected all of us, and made sure no one knew, but instead I let my misdeeds spill from my mouth like the toxic water surrounding me now from the acid pools.

Our once close relationship, ruined. The only human I ever loved, and now she's safe in a colony on Red Earth, and I'll never see her again. So sure, gut yourself and spill open your secrets, but don't expect anyone to walk away from the situation feeling any better.

Someone yells at me to hurry up, and I shake my head clear of the torment. I zigzag around the field of smallish volcanoes and settle between piles of red rock that rise like a wall, separating me from the others. Dirt fields encompass the whole planet, pockmarked with the acid puddles and one larger acid lake down past the volcanoes. Gnarled crimson plants twist up from the dirt that surrounds toxic water. Occasionally the volcanoes spew ash and rock, small threats to remind us they could wipe us out at any moment. Luckily, we haven't encountered any life-threatening eruptions, but I wonder how long that could continue. Surely, it's only a matter of time before something violent erupts from the wide necks of these angry mountains. Most resemble smaller versions of Earth's cinder cone volcanoes. Perhaps it's their size that keeps us from feeling like they'll eradicate us, but there are so many of them. Fields of deep craters and lava domes, of burbling gases beneath the rocky land and a constant stream of gurgling bubbles from the fetid ponds. Everything on Sulfur Planet is a threat, but maybe like me, the others don't care. The planet is our very own death wish; we just have to keep working until oblivion takes us home.

Though maybe this is already oblivion. Every day remains the same. I get up, walk down to the volcano field, chip away at the sulfur composites, and then on the way back up the hill after our work for the day is done, I stop at the biggest acid lake. Stare into it, hypnotized. Something waits down there, in those depths none of us could ever reach. I know it does, but the few times I've tried to tell the crew, they look at me like I've grown another head, and really, growing another head seems plausible on this planet. Who knows what effects these gases and this new air will have on our human bodies in the long run?

My thoughts tangle as I turn away and retreat back into the habitat, too tired to eat with the others or fish out any stowed snacks from my backpack. My nightmares have continued to worsen, but this kind of exhaustion from mining isn't fightable. I always slip into sleep. And dark reminders of my past, of my present, they slip into those twisted dreams with me.

Sunrise on our sulfuric world is perhaps the best time of day and easily the most beautiful thing about this arid, odd place. Tones of tangerine sorbet awaken the planet, and I rise with my fellow workers to greet the day. Dreams from last night linger, vivid in my mind. I wonder if something in the air here causes that, or maybe I'm looking for excuses for why my brain so clearly recalls all that blood and screaming.

The images are usually the same: two babies crying, the tortured look on my sister's face from those last days on Earth, both of our hands smeared crimson, and then a cutscene takes me away to Sulfur Planet's acid lake. It all coagulates in my sleeping mind like an enigmatic puzzle. Is my subconscious telling me to end it all, to walk into those deadly waters and let my entire mass dissolve? Maybe that's the sum of my worth, a body destined for disappearance in the lethal lake.

One of the other women calls my name. I let the dream images fizzle out and then follow her into a neighboring tent shaped like a big igloo for a quick, bland breakfast. The sky morphs into brighter orange, and I set off to work, noting today is Friday at last. We only receive weekends off, but there isn't much else to do or explore on a planet like this, so we usually end up working anyway to pass the time. Sometimes I sleep, though, spend the whole Saturday curled up, daydreaming about what freedom might someday look like. My body aches and begs for rest, but my poor limbs, with their many bruises, scrapes, and burns, will have to wait for a few more hours until I can collapse once again onto the lumpy bed and sleep away the exhaustion.

Blue flames spark all across the fields from the restless gases beneath our steps. Between those sparks remains silence. There is no time for small talk, plus none of us have the energy for casual conversation. We've been here for several months, but as hard as I think, I can't remember the exact length of time. When did our pod full of workers who signed up to mine on this desolate planet even land? Static buzzes in my brain as I try to remember. It might be possible to trade jobs with workers on neighboring planets, but we so rarely have contact with anyone besides the supply ship. They never stay to chat, just take the sulfur, leave the rations, and depart.

Maybe that's all they cared about because that's what they were paid to do—like how their bosses likely don't care about the lonely people on Sulfur Planet. We needed to gather the precious element that they manufactured into batteries, fertilizers, even makeup. Such important things to keep their colonies on Red Earth sustained. So, what did it matter how any of the workers feel? So long as we keep loading up the baskets, keep the supply going. The others, none of them would last two seconds here doing what we do. One inhale of the prevalent rotten egg smell emitting from the sulfur—a stench I'm so used to I don't even notice it anymore—and they would all scatter like fearful flies.

The first few days after we all arrived, I spent so long chatting with the others. We still felt human then, but now we all merely exist like clones more than as individuals. But we had talked, noted the strange colors and smells of the planet, exchanged stories of our lives and pasts—if we had anyone waiting for us on Red Earth, if we were ever able to recolonize there with the others. Many of us had no one, but so many others did, and it broke my heart every time I thought too long of how they'd likely never see their families and friends again.

I told the others as much as I could. Some things were too twisted to blab out to strangers. It tempted me often, though, to just say, "Hello, how are you? What was your past like? Oh, me? Well, I almost died a few times because I overdosed on the drugs they gave us to evolve our bodies to adjust to space travel. I should have never been given such a high dosage in the first place because of some weirdness in my body. When I couldn't get clean and had no more money, I desperately fell into the wrong crowd, who turned out to be stealing babies to take to Red Earth with them for who fucking knows why, and I stole my sister's three-month-old son to sell to these guys so I could buy enough drugs to finally end myself completely."

I can't imagine that conversation going well with anyone,

let alone a group of hardened miners, of poor folks like me with no other options… Even they wouldn't sink as low as I had. The story gets worse, of course, because Lori found me with drugs and her baby, but I've blocked out so much of that painful confrontation. I'm not sure if I remember it correctly at all anymore. I can barely recall what my sister's face looks like, other than the pain in her eyes that night.

I wish I had better memories to carry me through each day. Small comfort stems from the fact that I'm not alone in my recovery. Hell, I'm not even the only person on Sulfur Planet to have gone through the addiction to SpaceVex. The drug was said to be safe for most, something that would strengthen our lungs and immune systems, prepare us for the kind of travel most of us never dared dream of. Why some ended up deeply addicted, unable to shake the way those black capsules with specks like glowing stars made us feel, no one ever figured it out. No one cared enough to, when the majority of people felt fine. The governments, scientists, and pharmaceutical companies claimed it to be a mystery.

Liars. They knew. For whatever reason, when I swallowed those pills, it made the burning Earth and all that terror disappear. Transported me to a higher place in my mind where nothing could touch me, where no one could reach me. I became one with the stars, a shimmering light among a dark sky surrounded by others like me. Beautiful, invincible, a forever constant of something that sparkled truer than the North Star.

When the high faded away, I fell back into the trash reality of a dying planet. Desperate to escape my own head, I sold everything. I would have sold my own soul if it meant getting my hands on those drugs sooner. After I did pay for more SpaceVex, I had nothing left. Lori had her second baby, and I made the mistake of mentioning my status as an aunt to the wrong ears. To someone who promised me unlimited amounts of what I sought if I delivered something to him. Stealing my sister's baby, it wasn't exactly something I could casually tell my coworkers on a foreign planet. And like I said, most of us barely talk to each other now anyway. Too tired. None of us are close enough to bleed open those still-raw wounds.

With the silence of voices around me, most of my company now comes in the form of volcano songs. The way ash sputters, the melody of flowing lava deep inside those craters, the toxic sonata of bubbling venom beneath the acid lake… These are the noises that ground my reality, keep me sane. Before we all drowned beneath exhaustion and quietness, one of my favorite coworkers, a man from Java who spent years of his life working in the sulfur mines of Indonesia, had the most fascinating stories. I asked him one day what he missed about that place compared to our new home. He told me of the native songbirds, how he missed their chirping. No birds here. No roaming tigers or silvery gibbons, no warty pigs or other creatures that teemed with life, but he remembered. He knew what life had been on Earth before we all destroyed it, let it burn.

No signs of life here on this desolate orange rock at all. Sometimes, though, I swore something moved, lurked in the shadows out of the corner of my eye. A feeling haunts me often, summoning me to stare into the acid lake every day. The strange ripples of light and heat that bubble from its algae-green surface. Smaller pools of toxic water linger at the bases of some volcanoes, with deeper craters embedded into the planet's surface, but they feel to me like minor distractions. No, something lingers beneath that lake, something we will never discover or find out. Something that learned to adapt and survive on this peculiar planet of sulfur.

The heat-resistant suit I wear as I begin my day's work protects me from the smoldering waves the volcanoes emit, but the clothing would do no good if I decided to take a swim in the lake. No one's tested that theory completely, but after we'd first arrived, a man named Davis toed around at the puddles with his steel-toed boot, and the water ate right through it. Davis at least kept his toes, though.

We all know the government could have granted us more gear or protection, more anything, but then again, it's unlikely they have anything in their stores that would truly shield us if one of the bigger volcanoes erupts one day. Still, the threat of lava doesn't take up as much space in my thoughts as what I fear lingers beneath the acid. My dreams keep taking me there more frequently. A warning of some kind—one that I could not explain or put into words to the others. The uneasiness churning through my stomach every time I glance at those sticky waters… It's only a matter of time until what lurks beneath reveals itself with shuddering clarity.

With nothing else to do, I work through the apprehension of dread. It's easy to tell who worked the sulfur mines before coming to this planet. The men with broken-down bodies and twisted spines. Laborers who bore blisters on their shoulders from carrying hundreds of pounds of the devil's gold from the source to the base camps where they once worked and lived. I used to watch them in the morning as they'd button protective suits over gnarled bodies, marred skin abounding. A glimpse of what could have been the future for my body, of what might yet tear it apart. The work they'd done for years, and that their fathers and grandfathers did for years before them, the necessity of it carrying on throughout time and now space; yet of all the incredible technology we possessed, sulfur mining still depended on a person's strength and resilience.

Why had modernity never found a home there, or a way to relieve the burdens of these people as the rest of the world continued to pretend they did not exist? Invisible workers who retrieved elements from the core of dangerous places. All the exploitation of poverty, of people the wealthy would never care about.

When I arrived here, my intent to punish myself outweighed all other feelings, but as I watch broken people go to work beside me, beside others destitute like me, displaced humans of all backgrounds and cultures, different identities blurring out into nothing because all that matters here is if you can do the work, I wonder: Will my body bend and reshape like the old miners' bodies have? I study my hands, my arms, feel the strength in each limb despite the pain and aches from my exhaustion. Compared to how I felt while dealing with the withdrawal from SpaceVex, I would take the fatigue any day. I may be stuck on Sulfur Planet for… well, forever, but having my awareness and lucidity back, not depending on something that altered the wires of my brain in such deeply disturbing ways, even if it prepared my body for this journey, it means everything to have that function restored.

Part of me, though, knows it only matters so much. I'll most likely work here until I die, or until something goes wrong and the planet kills me, kills us all. If our bodies quit one day, when we're too tired to carry on, will the guards dispose of us then, throw us into a volcano or the acid lake?

Inside the volcano where I work, sulfur crystals glitter like sparkling bile around the cracks where gases release. Banks of bright yellow line up around the jutting insides of volcanic rock and also around holes in the ground throughout the entire volcano field. The purity of such yellow blinds me at first, like looking into the sun, but other times I'm reminded of decay. Our gear keeps us cool, so the comfort of working in daylight doesn't leave us blistering through our skin from the volcanic temperatures. A former miner from Earth named Ahmad once told me that they could only ever work at night to collect sulfur. Darkness was needed then to stifle the terrible heat, but even then, conditions drove workers to both illness and madness. All these sulfurous gases, our face shields may protect us from breathing them in, but back on Earth, the workers were never offered anything. I can only imagine how their lungs burned, how their insides shriveled like disintegrating coal from all the toxins they'd breathed in.

Metal pole in hand, I slam the archaic weapon down to break the sulfur into manageable slabs. Golden chunks drop down, thick and resilient. It's strange how advanced Earth became, yet here I am with a simple pole, chipping away at the stalactites that loom down. We should have some fancy gadget that makes this all so much easier, but it seems all the best technology went to those who could afford it in the first place. The rest of us are left behind, mining on a barely known planet just to send money to our loved ones or keep ourselves afloat, though maybe some of the workers here are like me. We'll work, sure, but if we die in the process, it won't feel like the worst thing. I already did the worst things, and death seems like the next logical step.

Something yips behind me, but I don't have to turn and look to know what it is. The damned thing is going to have to wait another minute until my baskets are full. The most helpful equipment the governments brought us in their temporary alliance are robotic creatures that look a bit like wide dogs with giant metal baskets on their backs. The robo-pups, such a generous gift, I think, and roll my eyes. Everything else here is archaic, and the robots only help save us from having to haul the hundreds of pounds of sulfur on our tired backs. A preventative measure to hopefully promise that our spines won't end up as dented and twisted as the men from Earth who had to do all of this without an ounce of government technology, because when did the powerful ever give a damn until the Earth burnt up?

I transfer the lumps into baskets, and once each basket is full to the brim, I move it outside the volcano for the robo-pup to grab and store, leaving me with free baskets to refill over and over, until the light gets low and it's time to go back inside the habitat.

Someone calls my name, but it echoes around the dense rock in a chorus of "Cora, Cora, Cora." No one stands near me at all; there are so many volcanoes and banks of sulfur here that we usually have the option of working alone in a spot if we don't feel like being around others for the day. I often choose the solitary option.

The echoing of my name continues, bounces from the rocks in a shuddering invitation for me to turn around and look at something. I don't turn back. I can't. Something is out there, waiting for me to discover it at last and look into its eyes. And I already know exactly where I'll go when the shift ends and the sky turns into those seductive burnt-orange tones.

The lake. It's always the lake asking me to stay for a while.

I concentrate on work, ban my thoughts from jittering around all loose in my head. Focus. Eyes on the sulfur, those odorous yolky heaps of elements that need mined because this is my destiny. I don't stop.

I can't. Even one second away from swinging the pole and beating down those crystals is a second too long, a second that invites my brain to retrace the steps of my nightmares.

Crying babies. Shadows. My sister's broken face. Blood. The acid lake. Images repeat on a cycle over and over again. And over and over I swing the pole, break the sulfur, load up the baskets. Whistle a distorted tune beneath my face shield.

The work and the light do not last forever. After hours that seem like only seconds to me, another worker is tapping my shoulder, telling me it's time to quit for the day. My muscles thank me for stopping, but my brain knows better. It understands that a temptation greater than my own will against it is about to unfold. I walk with the others, my goggles sticking to my skin like sweaty suction cups. When we're farther away from the volcanic heat, I remove my shield and gently pull the goggles and mask from my clammy face.

Sulfurous gases ignite through the air, sparking out blue warnings. Waves of unease sink beneath my ribs like the ocean before a storm. Dread consumes my heart, drowns it beneath the unchangeable knowledge that I shouldn't be here. None of us should. I don't understand where the thought comes from, but it's there, a kind of deep comprehension that is unshakable in its finality.

The acid lake remains wedged between the volcano field's edge and an empty area of sharp rocks. As I move closer to the murky jade surface, something ripples from beneath. What's moving in there, down in those waters with unknown depths?

I stop and stare at the ripples, more of them. Concentrate. I'm vaguely aware of a shadow next to me, another woman from the mine. A worker I was almost close to before the exhaustion stopped us all from continuing to get close. If I was going to tell my secrets to anyone then, it would have been her, and now as I stare into the lake's dancing surface, I can't even remember the woman's name.

She grabs my arm, pulls me away from the bank of loose rock where I could have so easily slipped, could have fallen into the embrace of those toxic waters. Her goggles are still on, but beneath them I can see the furrowed brow, dark hair streaked with silver, sweat beading down from her forehead. The questioning gaze on her face asks me what am I doing, and I don't have to wait for her to speak to confirm that because I know that look so well. It's a look I've received my entire life.

I shake my arm out of my coworker's grasp and step away. Sizzling blue threats radiate from the burning gases and then onto the lake where the fire dances atop the surface. Others start calling our names, gather around and watch in the distance because it's time to go back into the habitat and enjoy our two days off, so what the hell are we doing down there?

Not now, a voice whispers in my head. Another time and everything will be discovered. I trust the voice, cast one more glance at the acid lake, and then follow the others up the rocky ledge, away from the volcano field and away from the secrets lurking beneath thick waters.

Blood. Shadows. Crying.

Same dreams, same images. I should know better than to hold any hope that my brain would gift me with a restful night free of night terrors, but hope is a tricky bastard. I sit up in my cot, recall the moment where the cutscene to the acid lake happens, but this time it lasted longer. Something talked to me from those depths, and I had talked back. Whispers, voices. It had all seemed so familiar. I desperately try to cling onto those fading moments of sleep and recollection, eager to remember what else transpired, but all I can envision is the rocky bank of the lake and garbled words that don't make sense any longer. I want to know. I need to understand.

It's Saturday, and I should stay here in the comfort of the habitat and rest all day with the others, but I see a few bored souls getting into their gear to go head into the volcano field and work to pass the time. I decide to join them, since it will look less suspicious if I work in the volcanoes near the acid lake rather than journey over to it for fun. I don't want the questions and stares until it's absolutely necessary. Until I solve the riddle my dark dreams keep asking of me.

I take my time, eat some of our terrible food, and then get ready. I lag behind the others, close enough to look like part of the crowd deciding to work, but still keeping a distance that I could blame on being tired, unsure of how much sulfur I really want to mine today.

I don't even make it into the volcano.

Electric bursts of flame are nothing new to see here as the sulfur gases burn, igniting the rocky planet into a sapphire blaze for a few seconds, but today the fire is everywhere. A conflagration of blue shoots up from all the cracks and craters below. I stand with the others and watch in awe, no one daring to step foot onto the stony field.

It ends like it began, sudden and without warning. No more flames. Mutters from the crowd around me, confused workers shifting their weight and holding loosely onto their metal poles and baskets. Next comes silence. An eerie quiet replaces the almost comforting white static of the sizzling flames. It's the kind of silence that I have heard once before, back on Earth. During those last few weeks while everyone was getting ready to board their pods and leave, there was a day I went for one final walk, took in the emptiness of what used to be. The remaining animals had been rounded up for an optimistic transport to Red Earth, and I wonder now how many survived the journey, how many will survive the new planet?

But the silence of that day… It chilled me unlike anything else, until now.

Solve the puzzle, I tell myself. This is just another piece of it. Bubbles from the lake. Blood. Shadows. Crying.

I know these images, and I know this torture because it is my nightly torture. I have to go to the lake. I have to end this.

Sulfur Planet trembles. Back on Earth, I experienced a few quakes; we all did, near those final weeks before we had to leave. The rumbling from beneath the rocks reminds me of that now, but I can tell this is worse. So much worse.

When it happens, I barely notice or register it as real because the scene of molten lava flowing up from the cracks in the rock field is too strange and surreal of a horror. People around me run, dart away from the fields and back up the ledge. But the lava isn't erupting from the mouths of volcanoes, it's all leaking upward, as if the sky is sucking it up in an upturned kind of rain. Reversed gravity? I don't know, but I keep moving, carefully inching my way down the ledge while everyone else runs back up.

They point, whisper. Ask each other questions of how this is possible.

They don't know what I do, do they? That anything is possible if we just…what? Another piece of the puzzle and I almost have the answer.

Come here, the acid lake whispers in my head, beckoning me nearer. The others don't pay attention as I walk closer; everyone is too fascinated by the lava. I approach the lake's edge just as the cascading magma rescinds its gentle upside-down waterfall flow and then shoots violently into the sky, exploding like fireworks from the old world. Molten sparks rain down around us, but as the people I've worked side by side with these past few months scream and scatter, I stand on the edge of the acid lake and wait for something that I cannot name. Something that has beckoned me here since we arrived.

Between beauty and terror, it calls to me. I stare into the lake thick with toxic waters and strange goo. No reflection shimmers back. In my head, I see the images clearer more than ever. Lori's tortured eyes when I took her back to where I'd traded her baby. The drugs. The money. Us trying to buy the baby back. Two men fighting us, but together, sisters sliced into those bellies and gutted the men. Our dad was a hunter, taught us how to gut and skin anything.

Blood on our hands. No one would care, because those last days of Earth held no laws. No jail. No punishment.

I remember two babies stashed away behind dead men, and then a third man came. Took away one baby and ran. Lori took the other baby, and it was not hers. Two sisters whispered that the baby looked similar to her son, that he would be her son now, that someone had to take care of him, anyway.

Whispers that no one else needed to know. Ever.

I fall to my knees near the acid lake, remembering, desperate to wash the blood off my hands, and I start to reach into the lake, but beneath the cauldron-like hollow of the caldera, darkness brews and simmers. Doomed secrets aching to make their truth known to everyone here, not just me. We all came with secrets, and the lake knows, as I know in my bones and within every molecule that more truth will be revealed if I keep going. If I dare to accept the gift that's being offered.

I keep watching as others scream, as fountains of lava spray around from the orange sky and burn through those so-called protective suits of my fellow workers, of people I almost called friends and still could someday if I make them understand, let them know what I know. The lava explosions from the sky continue, eat through suit and skin of a woman far up on the ledge, burning holes clean through her torso. Steaming flesh falls in the middle of the field. A man a few yards away from me yowls in agony as the lava corrodes through his thigh, exposing muscle and then bone. Stench of burning hair and meat in the air, and I recognize this as the future of all planets that humans touch.

I watch briefly in mild interest, but more bubbles burbling up from beneath the lake snap my attention back to those lethal waters. The strange figures from my dreams, mere outlines then, transform into full bodies. Their dark shapes become whole as they emerge from the lake. Creatures far beyond the wildest stretches of imagination. I'd envisioned something maybe comprised of scales that had adapted to the harsh reality of acid liquids, but the reality is worse.

Skin hangs from charred bones like tattered, bloody strips on meat racks. Glowing eyes and open mouths full of pointed red teeth adorn their faces. The slashed-up ribbons of skin radiate colors of sickly green. Is this the fate assigned to something that dwells so long in the extreme acidity of the lake and has the nerve to survive, to call it home?

I don't know where the robo-pups come from or why they're out this far near the lake, but one wanders too close to a creature. The acid monster makes quick work of dissolving the robot's body down into a liquid pool of silver, with sparking wires unspooling from the melted metal. Together, a group of the creatures retrieves the sulfur from the basket the robot carried, and they take the crystals back into the lake with them.

I realize they aren't monsters. They're protectors.

Phreatic eruptions burst from the field, lava shooting everywhere and threatening anyone without shelter, the creatures daring us all to step a little closer. I can see it in their eyes, hear their voices in my head.

All of these enigmas hidden in the blue acid lake… As if any of us ever dared to know or understand what truth waits beneath that fizzing surface. Would we have believed anyone if they told us monsters nested there, protecting the things we harvest?

Maybe not, or maybe they knew we were capable of believing such secrets, that no one would work here again if word got out, and so all those investors would rather gamble our lives away than tell us the truth—we meant nothing to them. And as I stared at the creatures, I knew they felt the same, so desperate to protect what was theirs.

Darkness falls, too early, but as more creatures emerge and stand silently around the lake, unmoving and observing the scenes play out, surely feeding on the secrets they sense as they did to me, I wonder why I'm the first to figure them out. Perhaps my history is the worst of all who are here, or maybe I just wanted to find something greater. Something to elevate us all. The nightscape glows with a crushed diamond sky across black velvet. Whispers dance throughout the dark as the fires cool and lava returns to its correct place below the rocky terrain.

The creatures do not speak, but one steps forward and tilts its head at me, and somehow without words I understand. Every thought and question echoes in my mind, perfectly clear. The creature grows curious, asks me what I am thinking about right now.

"My sister," I answer, my voice barely above a whisper.

A transformation, they offer.

All of our relatives from Earth, our friends and family and those who once loved us, they either let us come here, made us, or just didn't care, but they could never predict what would happen next.

But I knew. The creatures have been showing me for weeks, maybe even months, in my dreams, between all my guilt of theft and murder and kidnapping.

We were to evolve.

I made a liar out of my honest sister. Helped her convince the others that, yes, this was her baby. Had always been her baby. That her reckless addict of a sister helped her get the baby back…

I didn't think I had anything left to offer Lori to make up for what I did, but now I do. I will.

I can offer evolution. We all can.

The creatures tilt their heads, open their sharp mouths where a black vortex spins inside in place of tongues, and they screech into the night. A screech that promises all of my guilt will end. That I'm not to blame for something a dying government made me take, got me hooked on, something that shook my whole world into crumbling pieces, chewed at me until I was nothing but crumbs, waiting for someone to help, but everyone was too busy selling and trading off assets and bargaining for things on the new planet, too busy getting their private pods ready to travel into space, and I would have been left behind to melt away on Earth if it hadn't been for the work on Sulfur Planet. I was always meant to come here.

We all would have died, finally gotten to see with our own damned eyes how Earth ended in a blaze, swallowed by the sun's unapologetic rage.

But I still have my rage. We all do, and I know as the creatures step forward, find the others and take them here, that they will help us see the power of our once forgotten fire. Help us use the kindling lying dormant in our bodies, because we deserve life, too.

I will show my fellow residents of Sulfur Planet that there is nothing to fear. I go first, hoping they will follow me as the creatures reach out, guide me into the lake. One final payment, one final transformation. We will emerge like them, be more adept to this world and other worlds. The colonizers on Red Earth, we will invite them next.

Lori, I will find you. I will give you one last apology to atone for my mistakes. A gift, a transformation.

Evolution is not always pretty, Lori, but we will be family again. Forever.

GARDENING BY THE MOON: A HOW-TO GUIDE

To garden by the moon—an idea that has been around for centuries and still holds a mystical beauty. In fact, using moon-phases is an excellent way to plan a healthy garden. Below you will find our guide to May, which includes the all-important Moon Feast!

May 1st: Sterilize. Good day for killing pests. Check plants and crops thoroughly, from root hair to stem to flower, if applicable. Remember to check teeth for any infections. **2nd–3rd:** Bad time for planting. Second day is best for carving idols for Moon Feast. Allow plants to calm after previous inspections. They tend to be skittish around this time. **4th–5th:** Favorable day for planting late bloomers; inspect crops, choose runts of the litter to give them a chance to grow. Under the age of five works best. Separating from parent crop will be difficult. Recommend strong pruning saw like carbon steel blade. **6th–7th:** Fine day for transplanting sprouts. Keep away from parent crops. Remember the massacre from last year? You don't want to become a victim at the tendril-hands of your plants, and they're quite protective of sprouts. Best removed, then transplanted at late hours. Quickly.

8th–9th: Check for rotting seeds and saplings. Some pests reside in blood and organs, so the rot doesn't show through right away. Removing only the rotting flesh does no good. Uproot entire sapling. Burn. We recommend the Smiling Ears earplugs—discreet, comfortable, and perfect for blocking out screaming plants. **10th–12th:** Good day for seedbeds. Second night will be clearest. Choose one plant to sacrifice to the moon. Bleed plant out over barren land. If you do not complete this step, you may not attend the Moon Feast, and it will be considered an act of treason. **13th–17th:** Barren period will continue as soil absorbs blood. Good time to take a short trip! Relax. Let the moon gods taste your sacrifice, and you will be rewarded. **18th–19th:** Favorable conditions for cultivating traitors. Those who committed the above act of treason will now be identifiable by silver glow emitting from irises. Pray to the moon gods, and they will help you round up the sacrifices. Second day is great for planting flower seeds! **20th–22nd:** Deliver carved idols to your local township's shrines. Clear days, best for mulching. Once their middles spread roots, crops tend to sink into dirt, keeping waste below ground. We recommend collecting waste from your crops before they're planted too deep. Recycle into the mulch. Healthy soil leads to healthy plants.

23rd–24th: Moon Feast! Celebrate the first day with food, family, and friends. Gather at sunrise on the second day. All gardeners must observe the sacrifice of traitors. Special seeds offered for every traitor you bring in. **25th–26th:** Storms expected. Take precautions. The flesh is still fragile and will need to be covered during heavy rains. **27th–28th:** Favorable conditions for pruning the dermis-leaves. Check on new sprouts. Premature stem bleeding can be sign of infection. **29th–30th:** If you were lucky enough to get those special seeds, plant them during these days. The human-ivy hybrids favor shade, while the skin-tulips flourish in sun. Stay tuned as we head into our June guide!

AFTER THE TWILIGHT FADES

Emilia stands in the field, bewitched by the blue haze of an early evening. Fur like brown rust contrasts against the dusk. She catches the fox in her peripheral, only for a moment before it disappears into the woods. A dense population of trees stand guard at the end of the field, and it would be so easy to slip into the wilderness and never return. She considers following the fox and vanishing into the twilight with crepuscular animals. A nighttime hunt, the excitement and energy it must bring—when was the last time she felt that alive?

She'd have to pass on hunting birds, though, for she loved them too dearly. Her dream as a child was to grow up and have wings, to fly away into the horizon. Instead, growing up had only brought the death of dreams.

While she doesn't mind finding herself in this delicate moment before nighttime falls, she wonders how she got here.

The field belongs to her closest neighbor, which still requires a half mile of walking. The fox distracted her, but it wasn't a part of her original motive for trekking through overgrown weeds and brambles.

She closes her eyes, searches through the fault lines of her memory.

The light, she remembers. Something fell from the sky.

She'd been sitting alone on the porch, rocking in the wicker chair, which she'd sooner burn, but Dylan cherished the ugly rocker. Whatever Dylan loved always took precedence over her own distaste. Daydreams of incinerating furniture left her thoughts when she noticed the object in the sky. The trajectory was so close, and its descent ended somewhere near the field and trees. Her house on the hill provided a good view, so she'd set off to find the rock or debris, or otherwise.

She doesn't remember actually leaving the porch, though, or putting on her shoes, yet she's done both. Before the distraction of the fox, she'd been fixated on the memory of the object's flaming tail, how it morphed from golden to bright green. An ethereal green.

Ethereal. Not a word she uses a lot, but it blooms into her brain before she has much time to consider the choice.

She stands on the edge of the field, peering into the labyrinth of trees. Light footsteps carry her across a dirt trail, and not once does she think about which direction to turn. An invisible string pulls between her and whatever has fallen, and she listens to its summons. Laughter so joyous, she thinks it's emitting from the trees, but she is the source. When was the last time she laughed so genuinely?

And to think, the cause is this small rock, shimmering in the woods. At first, it looks like a small rubber ball, no bigger than her closed fist. She steps closer and then examines the craggy surface. It isn't perfectly round, but it's close. Of all the photos she's glimpsed through on the internet of meteorites, they've never looked so spherical. They always appeared to be uneven slabs, like any old rock.

And none of them were ever glowing green after their fall, at least not that she'd read about. The same luminosity she witnessed from the sky radiates again, this time from the meteorite's center. Around the small sphere, grass smolders. Dying wisps of smoke curl up and disappear into the darkening twilight. No fire danger, she assesses, but the autumn blades have been reduced to curled, black strands. The grass smells more like burnt hair than foliage, and it forms a dark halo around the cosmic rock.

The intensity of its glow, like an ember refusing to die out, excites nerves within Emilia. Such curiosity hasn't come to her in ages. She kneels in front of the rock, letting the trees surround her like a forested chapel.

She doesn't pray, but she does whisper. Maybe if she tells the rock a secret, it will tell her one back. The divinity of this uneven sphere invites her to crawl closer. The green of it nearly corrodes her vision.

Or maybe it's radioactive and will kill her.

Either way, her fingers stretch out and trace over small bumps on the surface. Glassy dewdrops. How satisfying they feel as she runs the pads of her fingers across each tiny protuberance. This first contact of skin and celestial rock is sacred. Oils from her hand meet the warm light of the meteorite. Microbes mingle and dance. A smile stretches on Emilia's face, tugging at muscles she hasn't used in so long. The delight of a true grin almost makes her cry.

Any thought of the meteorite harboring contamination leaves her suspicions. The rock emanates balance and trust. The grace of its power transfers into her very bones.

The meteorite murmurs to her: *What do you want?*

A crackle of electricity in the air. She almost responds with the wish to be numb, but numbness and detachment have already been a part of her life for years. What she wants now is to feel everything. Perhaps then, she could understand the love others carry for her. Love has been a cold void, and she wishes to embrace its warmth and peace again. The wish is about more than love, though. Every day, she goes through the motions of being a human, but it's like watching a movie of herself. She knows the script, the words to recite to make her a good worker, a good wife, a good whatever, but there's no satisfaction. No fulfillment. The rock hums as her fingers trace around its crevices, as if showing her it understands. It knows she's lived in this gray state of mind and heart for long enough.

Speaking of love, look at Dylan. How he barrels down the field, waving his arms like one of those silly inflatable tube guys outside of a car dealership. Her husband yells across the field as he nears the trees.

"Don't touch it!" His voice reaches her, but poor Dylan, it's too late. She's already caressed every inch of smoothness, every contrasting crag and color. He moves toward her still, as if he can save his wife, but then he becomes suspended in time. This moment is just for them, Emilia and the rock.

"I want to feel every moment, every emotion. I want to connect to the very core of this universe," she confesses, and the rock absorbs her words with the finality of sealing a wish in wax.

Time shifts again with a green blink in the sky. Dylan lurches forward, then kneels beside her. His lips move fast, and she cannot process his words.

"Emilia?" Fear reflects in his big eyes with an endless ocean of concern.

She grips the meteorite harder, afraid Dylan will pry it from her fingers. The rock heats up to a gentle burn, then sears into her flesh with a kind of ecstasy. She falls under its trance and lets the blister slither beneath every inch of skin. If this is the granting of her wish, then she wonders what consequences will follow.

Double irises with functioning pupils. She looks up the technical name: True polycoria.

It happened after the meteorite encounter. She'd been so out of it, wandering the house like a listless spirit. Dylan had walked over to her, arms outstretched as he went in for a hug, and then he'd gasped in such a dramatic way, Emilia laughed for the first time since she'd grinned at the rock in the woods, at least until she went over to the bathroom mirror to see what the gasp was all about.

That was two days ago, when the pupils started to form. Today, the amber of her irises has fully doubled, and her pupils reflect a blackness she imagines can be found at the bottoms of oceans, or in the vast nothingness of space. Which is she bound for, drowning or drifting away into the unknown?

True polycoria. A rare condition, but not impossible.

The words echo in her thoughts. When she tries to speak aloud, her words die in the cobwebs of her throat. Her blood demands quiet, and her only choice is to obey.

Since that evening in the woods, the rock relinquished its hold on her palm, and now it rests peacefully on the living room coffee table. Emilia spends most of her days sitting on the couch, staring at it. Thinking. She also experiments with the eye development. They seem to be operating independently and granting her an odd ability to focus on four different objects at once.

She turns her left hand over. In addition to multiple pupils, the meteorite left its mark on her palm with small scars. The meat of her hand and all the way up to her fingertips is decorated with pinpricks of faded purple dots.

A few more days pass, and then there is a woman who looks so much like Emilia, standing in the living room. Holly cries and doesn't try to hide her worry like Dylan thinks he's doing, but Emilia always could see through that.

There is a press of warmth as Holly hugs her, and Emilia wishes her heart would unthaw, but the stillness of her body now must be like hugging a statue. Her sister retreats into the kitchen with Dylan, where he's been making smoothies for the week. Emilia can slowly slurp them down, but otherwise, she's been unable to open her mouth and chew and eat. The very thought exhausts her.

Dylan's low voice carries out to the living room as he tells Holly about the useless visit from the family doctor. She barely remembers the white-bearded figure. He'd asked some questions, checked her blood pressure, looked in her ears, then left.

"Can you hear me?" Holly emerges from the kitchen and sits next to Emilia on the sagging gray sofa.

Yes, of course. The words don't leave Emilia's lips. Instead, she blinks twice at Holly.

Her sister smiles, then whispers, "You can."

It's a game from their childhood. They had discovered the best way to irritate their mother was refusing to speak with words. Emilia and Holly invented their own language in a series of blinks, knocks, stomps, and other noises. They'd giggle between chirps and snaps, and they'd even taught their two pet parakeets some of the more ridiculous sounds. It took several weeks, but Fern and Spangle both learned a few noises, including the *ding* of the kitchen timer Emilia and Holly used to end their wordless conversations. She'd loved them fiercely. Fern with his pretty jade feathers, and Spangle with the purple-black specks around his face. When everyone called her difficult to deal with, even in childhood, the birds never judged her.

"I have an idea," Holly says, and the young woman radiates a nervous energy Emilia recognizes all too well. Whatever she is going to suggest, Dylan most likely won't agree with, and Holly knows, too, but it won't stop her.

"What is it?" Dylan's voice is guarded as he asks the question.

"My friend knows a hypnotist. A good one, I promise."

"Really? That's your solution?"

"Hey," Holly protests. "She helped my friend quit smoking. Give her a chance."

They argue quietly, desperation making itself known, and Emilia is touched by how much they care. She zones out, though, lets them make this decision on her behalf. Her focus is on the meteorite. So close, yet she cannot pick it up off of the coffee table. When Dylan and Holly turn to go back into the kitchen, the rock glows in a prism of burning green.

Ethereal, Emilia thinks.

You will be, too, the rock hums back.

The hypnotist arrives the next day. Holly remarks on how kind the doctor is to make this house call, but Dylan only nods. He lingers by the door, away from the rest of them as he watches.

"I'm so glad you got my voicemail," Holly says. Her breath comes out in a nervous rush. "I wasn't sure if I called the right number."

Come over here, Emilia wishes to tell her husband. *Hold my hand.*

"This is my sister, Emilia." Holly leads the woman over to the couch, and the hypnotist sits next to her rather than taking the chair across from her.

"Hello, Emilia. I'm Dr. Aelina."

She blinks once in a version of saying hello, but then she can't stop staring at the doctor. The woman is striking, perhaps ten years older than Emilia, and with hair the color of a sand dune. Black liner contrasts with the intense emerald eyes.

"And this is the rock." Holly points to the meteorite. No one has touched it since Emilia placed it on the coffee table.

"Oh, how lovely. So unique." Dr. Aelina admires the rock, studies it from afar. She doesn't pick it up, but her fingers twitch. Does she sense it, how the rock whispers? "An amazing lunar meteorite sample. I've never seen one quite like that."

"You can tell it's from the moon?" Holly settles into the armchair across from Emilia.

"Well, *a* moon. Not necessarily ours."

Dylan snorts and paces across the room. "Is that even possible? And what are you, a hypnotist *and* an expert in cosmic rocks?"

"Dylan," Holly seethes, and Emilia is grateful her sister can show anger on her behalf. She wants to ask Dylan what the hell his problem is, but she cannot speak. Cannot move. If only she could rip her skin away and crawl out of its sticky, stinking mess.

Dr. Aelina smiles. Her lips glisten with a clear gloss, and it makes Emilia think of glass. As if those lips could fracture and shatter.

"It's quite alright. He's allowed to question my hobbies." She turns her scorching gaze toward Dylan. "I am many things. Today, though, I am someone who is going to help Emilia. If that's okay with you?"

Dylan clears his throat, perhaps searching for an apology. "I don't know a lot of women who are hypnotists."

The doctor arches an eyebrow. "Maybe you just don't know a lot of women."

Dylan withers under her scrutiny, and some sense of satisfaction blooms in Emilia as she watches him retreat. The woman focuses again solely on Emilia, and she lets herself sink into the doctor's soothing voice.

"Together, we will wade through the darkness. We will find what's troubling you and keeping your tongue a prisoner. You will emerge stronger, brighter than ever before."

How does she know of the darkness? It's been growing heavier in Emilia's thoughts, like a great storm cloud come to chase all sunlight away. There were times where she could hold onto memories and moments with perfect clarity, as if her wish had truly come true to feel an omnipresence. Then, rolling black clouds shook her with thunderous nothing. Heartbeats slowed, and her veins operated in dizzying lightning strikes, whether to keep her alive or kill her, she wasn't sure.

Does Dr. Aelina sense it too, how Emilia's bones shift? How her sinews are rewiring? With every moment of stillness and silence, they alter a little more. Invisible. Her statuesque pose is their ruse, and she can tell no one.

"Can she write in this state?"

Dylan shakes his head. "We tried days ago. She refuses to hold the pen."

"That's not her fault." Holly bristles like an angry cat.

"Easy now, both of you rest," Dr. Aelina tells her audience. "Let me try a few things to help."

Hopefully help is a reality. Her whole mind seems off, like a clipped wire sparking at both ends.

"Emilia…" Dr. Aelina's voice is breathy and gentle. She likes the way her name sounds on the doctor's tongue. "Are you ready?"

She blinks twice.

"She's ready," Holly confirms.

"I'll tell you everything as I do it. I promise. No surprises here. I will explain each step." Dr. Aelina reaches for the lunar meteorite.

"Wait!" Dylan juts forward, panic in his voice. "Touching that is what drove Emilia into whatever state this is." He gestures at her like she's a catatonic zoo animal.

The hypnotist merely chuckles and then grabs the rock from the coffee table. "This item is harmless to me. Emilia's mental state is born from events much more complex than a meteorite."

A strangled noise dies in Dylan's throat.

"Focus on the meteorite," Dr. Aelina says. It's easy to follow this command. She has concentrated on little else. "I will keep the meteorite in my hands, safe. You are safe, too. Look at the glittering crags here. Let their gleam fill you with a sense of security."

Safe. She's always been safe. Nothing else. She wants more.

"When I touch your neck with my finger while saying 'numb,' your neck will go numb. You won't feel that spot at all, as if an anesthetic has been localized."

The pad of a finger applies pressure to Emilia's neck and rubs cold circles into the skin.

"Numb, numb," Dr. Aelina repeats.

A flash of bright green blazes in the room, and then Emilia falls into the darkest depths she's ever known.

Numbness spreads from the spot on her neck and encompasses her torso like being submerged in murky waters. Her head remains above the numbness. Earlier, she was aware of her hands, her fingers, the beat of her heart, but now she can only assume they are still there and functioning.

"Keep breathing," Dr. Aelina says. "The numbness won't steal your breath. Command your body to breathe, and your lungs will obey."

Emilia inhales and manages to suck in a breath, though her torso feels crushed.

"Your eyes are closed, and you're swallowed by darkness. Try to find a light there, no matter how small."

"This is ridiculous," Dylan mutters, but it seeps into the dim and threatens to shatter Emilia's meditation. Her darkness flickers at the edges. Out of place.

"Ignore the outside that threatens to pierce your world," Dr. Aelina continues, and her voice is so smooth it lulls Emilia back into tranquility. "Search through the dim. What can you find?"

She lifts her hands and tries to find a surface or wall in the black space. Are there objects here she could bump into or trip over, or is this place an empty vacuum?

There. A pinprick of light. It beams through the dark like a small laser.

Another dot. And another. Green streaks emit from a source, and when Emilia glances down, she sees the source is her palm. The strange purple scars left by the lunar meteorite have come to provide illumination.

Dr. Aelina whispers, and it's so intimate, Emilia is quite sure the doctor is talking to her in her head, not aloud.

"What do you see?"

Emilia's mouth opens, and for the first time in nearly two weeks, she speaks. Her voice is a dry crackle of static, but it'll do. "Green sparks. Who are you?"

"A friend. Now tell me, are you ready to follow the light, to feel its true burning? You've had a taste. Do you hunger for more?"

"What is this?" She rotates her hand, and the beams follow, shooting from the tiny scars like holes into another realm, but it comes from within her. What exactly has happened inside her body since she touched the meteorite?

"You will awaken when I count down from ten and press the rock to your neck."

"Wait. What did I just see?"

"The truth."

Her mouth seals shut again. The lights radiating from her palm fade, and she misses them in an instant. That light belongs to her, it found her, and now the hypnotist is taking it away.

Wait, wait, wait.

The countdown ends, and a smooth part of the lunar meteorite connects with the skin on Emilia's neck. Numbness dissolves, and she's back in the living room. Dylan and Holly gather closer and look at her with expectations written in the lines on their faces.

Emilia is so tired of expectations.

"Can you speak at all?" Dr. Aelina asks gently.

She tries, but her body disobeys the command.

"I can try another method. We need to dig deeper into what is causing Emilia so much pain."

"What pain?" Dylan crosses his arms and sounds like he's taking this a little too personally.

The hypnotist ignores him. "Holly, tell me about a happy childhood memory. What did she love to do as a kid, above all else?"

"Hmm," Holly says, taking her task seriously because Holly always took everything seriously, ever since they were in elementary school.

"We always liked to play together. We're two years apart, so we spent most of our childhood sharing toys and dreams and adventures. But it was the birds she always wanted to come home to the most. We had these two parakeets. Emilia used her allowance to buy books about owning birds, or to get them new toys. They were her world."

"What did they look like?"

"Green. Vibrant green. So pretty. They had some funny markings around their beaks. Emilia could get them to talk and do tricks, but they'd bite the rest of us. Fern and Spangle. Gosh, I haven't thought about them in years."

How is that possible? Emilia wishes she could ask. She thinks about them all the time, despite it being a decade since they were taken from her. She'd had Fern and Spangle from the time she was ten until she turned seventeen.

"A good memory, Holly. Thank you. Now, this next method can be a little dangerous. It applies vital-spot pressure, but I believe Emilia will respond well to it."

"What do you mean dangerous?"

"Not to worry, but tell me, does she have any heart conditions, high blood pressure, or ulcers?"

"No."

"Does she faint? Get nose bleeds?"

Holly's cellphone rings, and her cheeks go red. Emilia wishes she could laugh. Poor Holly, she always was easily prone to embarrassment.

"Excuse me," her sister says and dashes away into the kitchen.

Dylan answers the doctor's questions, but his voice is gruff. "No fainting. Nose bleeds have been rare."

Dr. Aelina shuffles closer, and then there's a cold forefinger and thumb on either side of Emilia's neck; she feels pressure and wonders if the woman will strangle the words out of her disobedient throat.

"Breathe deeply. Hold out your arms to your sides. Good. Now revolve them in a circular motion, clockwise."

Emilia does as instructed, and she's surprised her arms lift and rotate. Her limbs have felt like dried cement these past few days.

"You have been asleep for so long, now it is time to awaken, Emilia. Breathe. Keep moving your arms, yes like that. You are not a cog, not a machine. Soon, your body will be freer than it ever has been. You will look at the world with those beautiful eyes. The new vision, it's a gift."

"A gift? She gets some mutation from a space rock disease, and you call it a gift. I think it's time for you to go, *doctor*," Dylan says with no attempt to hide his venom. He never believed the universe could contain mystic secrets. Emilia had liked to believe in something greater out there, that nature contained its own magic and mysteries, but Dylan tried to squash those beliefs.

Her gaze falls to the tan carpet, with its uncomfortably stiff fibers. When they bought the house, she had dreams of ripping it out and repairing the hardwood underneath, but Dylan complained wooden floors would get too cold.

She keeps breathing, keeps moving her arms.

Footsteps echo on the carpet, and Emilia glances back up to see rage coloring Holly's cheeks, but Holly only glares at the hypnotist.

"Who are you?"

Dr. Aelina smiles. "I've told you my name."

Holly crosses her arms. "My friend called to let me know the hypnotist who helped him is sick today. She won't be able to make it over."

The smirk never vanishes from Dr. Aelina's face. "As much as I admire my colleague, this case was not for her. When I heard your voicemail on the office phone, I took the case in her place."

"There is no Dr. Aelina at that office. I checked. Get out." Holly marches forward with an angry Dylan at her side.

A force sends the pair backward. Emilia's sister bangs her closed fist on something invisible, separating them from coming any closer to the couch.

"I'm impressed," the doctor says with what sounds like genuine affection. "I didn't think you'd be able to put up a wall already, but look at that."

I did that? Her heart beats with the erraticism of a bird with mighty wings, trapped in a cage.

"Your energy is trying to protect you from what feeds off of it," Dr. Aelina says. "Like parasites. I know, that's not a very nice comparison for these two people who are your family, but sometimes love is like that. Sometimes love takes and takes without giving much back. Through the energy wall you've constructed, they can hear us, but we can't hear them."

Emilia centers herself. Breathes in. Breathes out. Moves her arms.

"Speak," the hypnotist gently coaxes.

Her throat is so dry, but through the painful gravel swallow of it, she squeaks out a few words.

"What is it?"

"The energy?" Her fingers cinch tighter at Emilia's throat, not once letting go. "Free your mind. Embrace the lunar meteorite's power. The world it came from, it calls to us now. Do you feel it?"

Emilia's mind swirls in cloudbursts of thought, weak attempts to understand the woman's words. She scans the room, all four pupils concentrating, looking for answers.

"Don't you see yet? You have been granted memories, both of love and pain. You hold the light of constellations in your palm. You've been chosen to ascend."

"Is there a choice?"

"Always. But why would you want to stay here? The lunar meteorite has forced rest upon your body, but it's been inside of you, making you stronger. Making you ready."

Emilia doesn't respond, but she keeps breathing, keeps moving her arms.

"Tell me more about the parakeets. What happened to them?" She pinches the nerves of Emilia's throat tighter.

Between ragged gasps, she talks. "My father. He killed them."

"I'm so sorry. Did Holly know what happened to Fern and Spangle?"

Tears sting her eyes at the mention of their names again. So small and innocent. How cruel, to not even stand a chance once her father decided he hated them. She'd been at school, expecting to come home to their happy squawks. Instead, silence and an empty cage greeted her.

"Our father manipulated her into keeping his secret. It wasn't her fault." An ache weighs so heavy in her arms. "I was mad at her for years, but I got older. Realized she was just a kid then, too. Our father was the only bastard to blame."

Holly sobs from behind the invisible wall, and Emilia cannot hear her, but she sees the red face and streaks of tears.

"What do you feel now?"

"Nothing. I tried anger. I tried love." She looks toward Dylan. "And it all added up to nothing."

"I sense more in you," Dr. Aelina says, and her intense gaze sends familiar electricity to sizzle in the air. "You harbor more pain toward both your husband and sister. What is it, are they sleeping together?"

The vibration of a laugh frees itself from Emilia's pinched throat. "No. That would be simpler, honestly. It would be a real reason to shut down and want to get away from everyone."

"What do you think your reason is?"

She hesitates. Her arms ache so much, and she nearly stops moving them, but the doctor glares and squeezes delicate throat skin. Holly keeps beating her fist against the unseen wall, harder and harder until blood drips down from scraped knuckles. The wall Emilia didn't even mean to conjure now makes her sister bleed. Is she doomed to bring hurt to herself and others, no matter where she goes?

"I'm a burden to them. Love isn't enough sometimes, is it? It can't always bring someone back from the ledge when they are so close to slipping off."

"What do *you* want?"

No one has asked her that question in years, not until the night in the woods two weeks ago when the rock said it to her. How beautiful the twilight had been before such a dark night.

"I'm so tired," she responds, "of feeling indebted to people when I can't love them back. Not truly. I wished upon this useless rock to change my numbness, but it was a foolish fantasy."

The ceiling shifts until it isn't a ceiling at all. In place of white plaster, storm clouds morph. Flashes of electricity spark between clouds.

"A lunar meteorite is not a wishing stone."

The words slash at her heart, but she's grateful to have the pain. It's better than the nothingness. Thunder from above rumbles, perhaps in agreement.

Dr. Aelina keeps one hand around Emilia's throat and then moves her free hand to place long, cool fingers against her cheek. The gentle touch is like ice against her boiling skin. Heat emits from inside Emilia, scorching away at the meat to make room for something else.

"The meteorite is much more powerful than any old wishing stone." Another green flash in the room. When the light fades, Emilia watches Holly silently screaming on the other side of the invisible barrier.

From the strange clouds above them, falls a rain of bright green feathers. How gently they drift down, like a soundless snow. Every single feather is splashed in blood, and metal fills the air with an acerbic tang.

It is the worst memory Emilia possesses, times a hundred. As if a thousand parakeets, a thousand Ferns and Spangles, had died gruesome deaths at the callous hands of her father and his knife—for no other reason than how much he hated to look at the birds. To listen to them sing. How much he hated seeing anything give Emilia happiness.

The grief, even from childhood, is overwhelming. Shocks of love and pain fry her nerves into frayed strings.

"They're draining you," the woman mutters. "Free yourself."

"I've always been told I'm the draining one. I'm the one who is too much." She keeps rotating her arms as the doctor squeezes her throat's pressure points. Tears fall freely down her warm cheeks, and bloodied feathers stick to the sweat of her skin.

All the exasperation she's been holding back pushes through her emotional dam. She doesn't have to stay here and be told she's too much to deal with. Maybe she can't even blame Holly and Dylan for not wanting to wallow with her in the gray landscape of her mind, but she didn't have to stay here, either.

"Is this what you wished for?" the woman asks, and Emilia supposes it is. Her own pain couples with the distraught nerves of her sister, the exasperation of her husband, and then she connects with the quiet of the trees outside. The calm of clouds as they drift across a sunset. It's almost the twilight hour, that beautiful blue moment before the night. Are the foxes waiting for her again? She senses them stalking prey in the woods, small paws on withering grass.

She doesn't remember the day disappearing. When Dr. Aelina arrived, the sun still blazed with yellow warmth outside of the living room windows on this unusually hot autumn day.

Now, bright light emits from her palm.

"A constellation. The lunar meteorite has given you a gift, stars in the shape of a parakeet."

It's an abstract shape, as many constellations are, but as the glow forms around her palm, the pinpricks make up a birdlike form.

"From your palm to the sky. Come with me to see it."

Feathers tornado around the room as Dr. Aelina stands up and holds out a hand, but her other hand is still secured around Emilia's throat. The blood coating each plume makes her stomach rumble, and she wonders in horror what kind of hunger this is?

"You've been famished so long," the woman comments, and her burning green eyes blaze. It's the same ethereal green of the lunar meteorite when it descended from the sky.

"What is happening?"

"Ascension, Emilia. As soon as you touched the lunar rock, you'd never be able to escape it. There is a price, though. You haven't been eating much while your body prepared, but you've rested long enough. I will guide you through this. No one will drain your energy, your life's essence, from you again."

Emilia chokes a little as pressure from the doctor's thumb and forefinger meets her throat stronger than before, and for a moment it's like a knife has sliced across her windpipe. Dizziness invades her senses, and the world goes sideways in a haze of static and gray hues.

"You are getting dizzy, but it's okay. You will ascend. Keep breathing deeply. Don't stop moving your arms. My name is Aelina, and I am here to guide you."

Dylan and Holly fade to smudges in her blurring vision; they're still trapped behind the barrier that keeps them silent. Perhaps they've always been there, unable to reach her.

"You are getting dizzy, but it's okay," Aelina repeats. "You will ascend. Breathe deeply. Don't stop moving your arms. Do as I tell you."

The pressure nearly causes her to black out, but she keeps breathing. Keeps moving. She gives into all of the pain, to how it promises ecstasy if she can see her way through this. Just like the elation the rock gifted her before.

"You are ascending. You are ascending. You are—"

Emilia bursts with light. She is a newborn star, gathering mass. Ascension becomes stellar evolution. She gushes with ethereal green, takes comfort in the way her bones shift and reassemble into a new Emilia.

Joyous laughter sounds from Aelina's throat, quite literally. The woman has another mouth there, smiling at the room from where there should be an esophagus. She shifts, too. Like Emilia, the woman has two pupils and irises. Unlike Emilia, rows of eyes cascade down Aelina's shoulders to the left and right arms, from neck to wrist.

"What do you see with your eyes, Aelina?"

The woman-creature takes Emilia's hand. "I see someone who is starving. Who experiences too much until it feels like nothing at all. Reclaim this hunger. The meteorite found you, and I will always find the meteorite. This sphere is special. It finds the broken and offers them a new life."

Emilia steps through the whirlwind of bloody feathers, and she lets the grief touch her new skin. It felt silly before, to so deeply grieve the birds she loved, but that was the first turning point in her life. She carried the ache and squashed it down. People she loved walked over her, or in front of her, but never beside her.

Emilia's four pupils focus on the unseeable wall, but as she embraces the meteorite's power, the energy becomes visible. A dark mist traps Dylan and Holly like animals in a pen. Energy glows tangible in the air. How deliciously it floats around them in prismatic swirls, but the doctor, or whatever Aaelina is, was right. Their energy is connected to Emilia's, feeding off of her, turning her once kaleidoscopic vitality into gray mist. No longer.

Emilia inhales the electric scent, and her stomach rumbles again.

Dylan screams, and Holly pleads, but she blocks it all out. Instead, she swallows their light whole and absorbs it into her still-changing body, not giving herself too much time to think about her actions. This is better.

Their every emotion becomes one with her, a knowledge in her blood she can keep forever. This is how she takes their love and gives it back, at last. From within her, they linger, always. With her past, her grief, and now her love. She plucks a green feather from the ground; like the others, it is speckled in blood.

She swallows that, too.

Emilia burns—whole and complete. Iridescence razors through her flesh, splits skin away like a baby bird cracking through the goop of an eggshell.

Sticky. Wet. She pushes through bones and meat, then grows too big for the room, the house, and the Earth. For a moment, she connects to every blade of grass, to each human heart no matter how broken, to any form of life on the planet she can grasp before it's time to move on.

Aelina leads her through the clouds above them that spin with fiery emerald light. Beyond time, to somewhere endless. She absorbs every sparking part of the journey along the way with a clarity so sharp, she lets tears of joy fall and sizzle against her skin. The lunar meteorite guides her as well as Aelina. As they ascend, Emilia glances back one last time to watch the twilight fade into night's totality.

A NOTE ABOUT REPRINTS

"Moonflowers" previously appeared in *The Horror Collection: Yellow Edition,* 2021

"With Radium on Her Lips" previously appeared in *Dark Dispatch Issue # 2: Deadly Love,* 2021

"As Humans Burn Beneath Us" previously appeared in *Field Notes from A Nightmare: An Anthology of Ecological Horror,* 2021

"Acidic Atonement on Sulfur Planet" previously appeared on *The Wicked Library* podcast, episode 1117, 2022

"The Viridescent Dark" previously appeared in *The First Five Minutes of the Apocalypse,* 2023

"After the Twilight Fades" previously appeared in *Apex Magazine* issue 136, 2023

"Cyanide Constellations" and "The Bones He Planted" previously appeared in *Seasons of Severance,* 2023.

"The Revenge of Rappaccini's Daughter", "Avian Eyes", "Gardening by Moon: A How-To Guide" and "A Haunting of Lawn Ornaments" are original to this collection.

ACKNOWLEDGMENTS

Short stories and poetry are the two main mediums that drew me so deeply into horror. Being able to share my debut fiction collection with readers is really a dream come true, and I'm very grateful to all of the editors and publishers who first published so many of these stories.

Thank you to Dark Matter INK and Rob Carroll for giving *Cyanide Constellations: And Other Stories* a wonderful home. I'm delighted to see the collection come to life (and with a fabulous cover by Devin Forst!).

I'm so grateful to have wonderful humans in my life who keep me sane, support my work, and constantly amaze me with their talents. A big thank you, thank you to Angela Sylvaine, Corey Niles, Megan Matejcic-Benson, Mike Arnzen, Nelson Pyles, Gwendolyn Kiste, Hailey Piper, Sam Brunke-Kervin, my always supportive sister and mom, and the HWA Pittsburgh Chapter crew.

—Sara Tantlinger

ABOUT THE AUTHOR

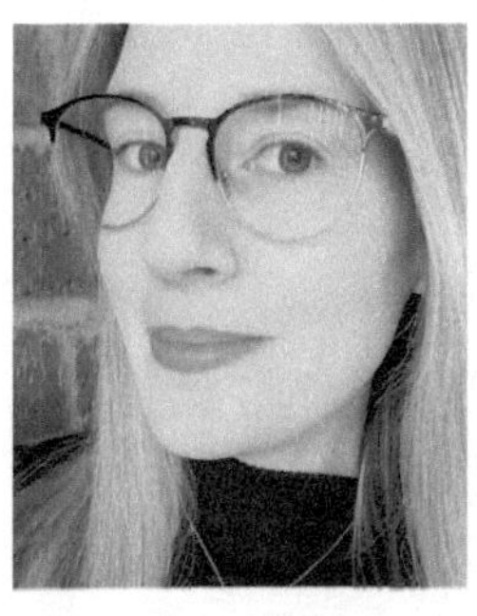 **Sara Tantlinger** is the Bram Stoker Award-winning author of *The Devil's Dreamland: Poetry Inspired by H.H. Holmes.* Her other books include *Cradleland of Parasites, Love for Slaughter, The Devil's City* (co-written with Matt Corley), and the Stoker-nominated novella *To Be Devoured.* She also edited the Stoker-nominated anthologies *Chromophobia* and *Not All Monsters.* She graduated from Seton Hill University with a BA in English literature and creative writing, and later with an MFA in Writing Popular Fiction. She is an active member of the HWA (Horror Writers Association) and the Pittsburgh HWA Chapter, which she co-founded.